Team Trouble at Dark Creek

NIKKI TATE

sononis
PRESS

Winlaw, British Columbia

National Library of Canada Cataloguing in Publication Data

Tate, Nikki, 1962-
    Team Trouble at Dark Creek

    (StableMates ; 2)
    ISBN 1-55039-076-7
I. Title. II. Series.
PS8589.A8735T32 1997   jC813'.54   C97-910669-9
PZ7.T2113Te 1997

First Printing: September 1997
Second Printing: November 2002

Sono Nis Press most gratefully acknowledges the support for our publishing
program provided by the Government of Canada through the Book
Publishing Industry Development Program (BPIDP), the Canada Council for
the Arts, and the British Columbia Arts Council.

Interior artwork *Face to Face* by:
Joan Larson CREEKSIDE STUDIO (250) 752-0395   www.joanlarson.com

Map by E. Colin Williams
Cover design by Jim Brennan

Published by
Sono Nis Press
Box 160
Winlaw, BC V0G 2J0
1-800-370-5228

Distributed in the U.S. by
Orca Book Publishers
Box 468
Custer, WA 98240-0468
1-800-210-5277

sononis@islandnet.com
www.islandnet.com/sononis/

PRINTED AND BOUND IN CANADA BY HOUGHTON BOSTON PRINTERS.

For Dani,
with thanks for her remarkable patience
and good humour

and for Hap and Mo,
that summer I was ten.

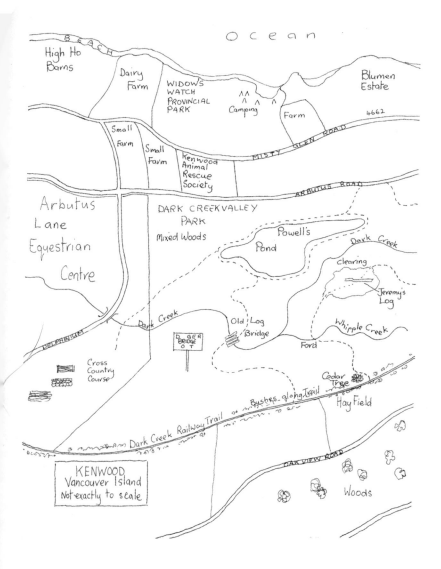

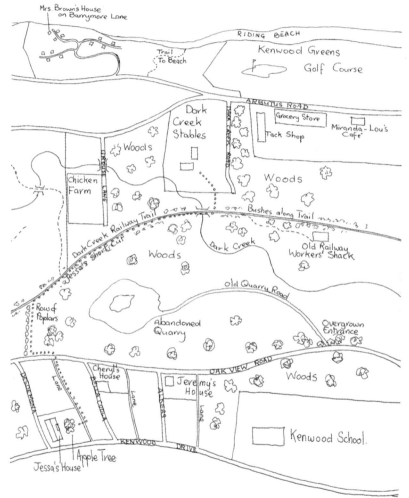

1

The horse seemed to form itself as Jessa's pen squiggled in the margin of her social studies notebook. A thick forelock tumbled into the stallion's dark eyes. She shaded the horse's neck and swept a smooth stroke up over his withers.

The school library was quiet. Every now and then a spatter of rain hit the high, narrow windows. It was too miserable to go outside to play.

"Jessa!" Cheryl Waters called loudly. Jessa's best friend raced across the school library, her orange-red hair sticking straight up. No matter what she did, Cheryl could never seem to get control of her thick mop. She wore it short, but even so, it always looked on the wild side.

"Shhh . . . you'll get us into trouble!" Jessa whispered, glancing uneasily towards the school librarian's desk. Mr. Birmingham either hadn't noticed Cheryl's outburst or had decided to ignore it.

"I have an idea," Cheryl whispered.

Jessa cringed inwardly. Cheryl's ideas were almost always outrageous. "This doesn't involve me, does it?"

"But of course!" Cheryl said, waving her pencil around

as if it were a magic wand. Cheryl wanted to be an actress. At the moment, she was working on finding dramatic hand gestures to accompany every word she spoke.

Jessa wondered whether it would ever get boring to live in a family like Cheryl's. Her parents ran a little theatre company. Cheryl's older brother, Anthony, went to university where, it seemed to Jessa, he was studying how to be eccentric. Anthony's girlfriend, Bernadette, was a student in the art department. She wanted to be a world-famous sculptor and live in New York.

Cheryl's house was always filled with costume racks and people with funny haircuts. Actors read scripts and were fitted for costumes in Cheryl's big kitchen. The living room had been the gathering place for the theatre people, but recently, Bernadette had taken over the space as a makeshift sculpture studio. Jessa had no idea what Cheryl's parents thought about *that*.

"So, I was thinking," Cheryl said, tapping her pencil against the bridge of her eyeglasses. "You know this social studies project we're supposed to do?"

Jessa nodded. It was worth a lot of marks. She hadn't even started yet. Every day after school she rushed down to Dark Creek Stables where she kept her pony, Rebel. She was trying her best to keep him in good shape right through the winter so he'd be ready for the earliest of the spring horse shows. These days, school work was sure getting in the way.

Jessa had no idea when she was going to find time to read two books about life in Victorian times. And *that* was only part one of the assignment. Then she had to write a journal as if she were someone living back then. If there was anything Jessa disliked more than social studies, it was writing.

Cheryl's face contorted and her eyes crossed.

"*What* are you doing?" Jessa asked.

"Trying to look intense and thoughtful," Cheryl answered. Then she rubbed her nose and looked a bit embarrassed.

"Actually," she said, "I poked myself with the pencil." She rolled her eyes dramatically. "Ouch!"

She blinked a couple of times before she went on.

"I was thinking we could act something out. We could write a play about two wealthy sisters who lived in a castle in England, or maybe Scotland. They could *both* be keeping journals. They don't realize it, but they are both in love with the same eligible bachelor."

Cheryl's voice was getting louder and louder.

"Shhh. I don't know if . . ."

Cheryl lowered her voice. "I already asked Mrs. Glocken and she said it would be fine. I have some great dresses from a production of *Little Women* we did a couple of years ago. I could be the older one because I'm a bit taller. . . ."

The class had been studying the Victorian era in social studies. Jessa liked looking at the pictures of the old-fashioned ladies wearing hats and bonnets and sitting primly in horse-drawn carriages.

"I don't think I want to get dressed up and read mushy stuff in front of the whole class," she said.

She wondered if Cheryl was ever going to do a *normal* school project.

"You mean, you're not going to work with me?"

Jessa shook her head and picked up her books.

"Oh, wonderful! Thanks so much for your support, *best* friend."

As it turned out, Jessa needn't have worried about working with Cheryl. At the end of social studies class that afternoon, Mrs. Glocken asked Jessa to stay behind for a few minutes.

Rachel Blumen whispered to her friend Sarah, "Oooh, Richardson's in trouble. . . ."

Rachel lived on a big horse farm not far from Dark Creek Stables. Her father bred Arabians. Jessa thought Rachel was a purebred snob.

As Cheryl gathered up her books she glared at Jessa.

"What's wrong with her?" mouthed Monika as Cheryl stalked out of the classroom.

Jessa shrugged. She wasn't sure if Monika meant Cheryl's strange behaviour or Mrs. Glocken's request for Jessa to stay behind after class. She certainly didn't want to talk about Cheryl and she had no idea what Mrs. Glocken's problem was.

She didn't have to wait long to find out. As soon as the last of her classmates had filed out of the room, her social studies teacher came right to the point.

"I understand your friend Cheryl would like you to do a play for the journal project—"

Jessa interrupted. "It's okay. I already said I didn't want to do it."

Mrs. Glocken looked taken aback.

"Oh, well, isn't that interesting. I suppose I'll have to call your mother back."

"What!?" It was Jessa's turn to be caught by surprise. "You called my mother?"

"No. She called me."

"Why!?"

"She's worried about your grades, Jessa. She thinks you're relying too heavily on Cheryl for help with your school work."

"But . . . I help her with her math in exchange," Jessa said.

"Yes. Your mother did say math was one subject she wasn't concerned about. It's funny, I was going to tell her I thought it was good for you to work with Cheryl. That girl has some very creative ideas."

"She does?"

"I really enjoy her projects."

"You do?" Jessa kicked herself for not taking Cheryl up on her offer.

"But, now that I think about it, maybe your mother has a point."

"She does?" Jessa felt totally confused.

"Let's see how you do on the journal project all on your own."

Since that was what Jessa had assumed she was supposed to do in the first place, she couldn't quite understand why she suddenly felt so disappointed. She wished she could sit down at Mrs. Glocken's desk and start the conversation all over again.

Mrs. Glocken smiled. "Let your imagination roam, Jessa. The idea is to try to take yourself back in time to that period, to think and feel how it must have been to be alive before the twentieth century.

"Remember, they had no electricity, no cars, no computer games, no fax machines. All the women wore long dresses and girls your age would have learned needlepoint."

Jessa nodded. She hoped the lecture would be over soon.

"Why don't you start by keeping a journal yourself and then think how a journal written a hundred years ago might have been different."

"Okay, I'll try," Jessa said glumly. The project would be a whole lot easier if it were about horses. Who cared about how people lived back then, anyway?

"Mom! How could you?" Jessa slammed the door and stormed into the house. She tossed her school bag down on the kitchen table. All the way home she had practised exactly what she was going to say to her mother.

"Jessa! Stop stomping around like that! Sit down and speak nicely if you have something to say to me."

Jessa marched out of the kitchen and threw herself into the old armchair in the living room. There was no way she was going to let her mother interfere in her life this way.

"I'm sitting!"

Her mother followed her in from the kitchen, where she had been potting houseplants on the counter. She wiped her hands carefully on an old towel.

When she spoke, her voice was cool and calm. "Now, Jessa Marie. What is this all about?"

Looking at her mother's solemn face, Jessa wished she had tried a more diplomatic approach. She stiffened in the armchair and managed to ask her question in a nearly normal tone of voice.

"Why did you phone Mrs. Glocken?" Just asking the question made her realize just how mad she was that her mother had snuck behind her back and called her teacher.

"Do I have to remind you about your last report card?"

Jessa glared silently at the pattern on the carpet. It was quite interesting how there were exactly twice as many beige fibres as dark brown.

"Jessa. Look at me when I'm speaking to you."

Jessa transferred her gaze to her mother's shirt. She didn't quite dare to set her blazing hazel eyes directly on her mother's face.

"Jessa, don't get so angry. I'm just worried that Cheryl is doing your homework for you."

"But, Mom. I wasn't even going to do her dumb idea for a project anyway!"

"So I heard. Mrs. Glocken phoned me after you left her class today."

Jessa scowled. She hated it when people talked about her behind her back. Especially her mother. Double especially her teachers. Triple especially when they talked to each other.

"Now. I don't want to have to resort to this, but if your marks don't improve I'll have to cut your riding back to weekends only."

"What!" Jessa burst out. "That's not fair! Rebel won't stay fit that way. We're in training!"

"I understand all that, Jessa. You know I have no problem with you riding as long as your marks are reasonable."

Jessa jumped out of the chair and headed for the living room door.

Jessa's mother rubbed her hands on her jeans. "I talked to Mrs. Bailey today and she understands completely. She said you could do extra barn chores in the Christmas holidays if you need time to get caught up on your school work before then."

"What! You called Mrs. Bailey?" Jessa was astounded. Her mother didn't usually interfere *this* much. Calling Mrs. Bailey to talk about homework problems was going too far. "Why don't you just call the whole world and tell everyone what a lousy student I am!"

"Jessa. Be sensible. You can't go through school with marks like—"

"But—"

"No buts. This is your last warning. Either you pull your marks up, starting with your social studies project, or you'll have to stop riding during the week. Do you understand?"

"Can I go to my room now?"

"Just a minute. When is your project due?"

"Not until after Christmas. I don't know why everyone is getting so excited," Jessa grumbled. "I have tons of time."

"Have you started your reading assignment yet?"

"No," Jessa said sullenly.

"Then I think your room would be a good place for you to go. You can get started tonight."

2

Jessa pedalled furiously down the long driveway at Dark Creek Stables. She clicked her stopwatch as her bike slid sideways to a stop in front of Rebel's paddock. Four minutes and fourteen seconds. Not quite a record.

Rebel poked his head over the fence and nickered a soft greeting. Jessa rubbed the white blaze on his forehead as she caught her breath. He nudged her elbow with his soft, black muzzle.

"Carrot? Is that what you're after?"

Rebel nodded and pushed his nose through the fence. His bottom lip flopped impatiently while Jessa pulled off one glove and fumbled for a carrot in her jacket pocket. At least Rebel wouldn't pick on her about homework.

"Here you go."

She patted her pony on the neck as he crunched. Jessa ran her hand under his thick black mane. His winter coat was already heavy.

"You need a new blanket, Rebel," Jessa said. His faded blue New Zealand rug was worn and patched. It was always hard to find money for horsey accessories. She hoped the old rug would last through the winter.

"I'll come back and get you in a few minutes," she said with a final pat.

Jessa pushed her bike to the shavings shed and leaned it against the back wall by the manure forks. Already the heat she had generated riding to the barn had gone. Even blowing into her gloves and clapping her hands together didn't help warm her chilled fingers. It was only the end of November but it seemed as though it had already been freezing for weeks.

Mrs. Bailey wasn't anywhere to be seen. Usually, Jessa could locate the older woman by listening for her loud but tuneless whistling.

The wheelbarrow used for taking hay out to the paddocks was turned upside down outside Jasmine's stall. A note was taped to it.

J-
This was half filled with water and left in the middle of the yard. What do you think happens to hay when it gets wet?   B. B.

Jessa blushed and looked up towards the house. She half expected to see Mrs. Bailey standing at her living room window with her arms crossed. But the windows in the log house were dark. She tore the note from the wheelbarrow, crumpled it up, and shoved it into her pocket.

Mrs. Bailey liked everything at Dark Creek to be done properly. It sometimes seemed that no matter how hard Jessa tried, Mrs. Bailey always found *something* wrong. Jessa sighed and started for the tack room.

A cup of steaming hot chocolate would help warm her up and make her feel better. After that, she would tack Rebel up and go out for a trail ride.

"So, I hear you're having trouble at school?"

It was too late for Jessa to hide. Mrs. Bailey was standing right in the middle of the tack room, almost as if she had been waiting in ambush.

Jessa stared at the floor. She wanted to grab her grooming kit and flee. But Mrs. Bailey had other ideas.

"Where do you think you'll wind up without a decent education? You'll wind up like me, shovelling out stalls when you should be sunning yourself in Florida in your old age. You wouldn't want that, would you?"

Grown-ups and their lectures. Very tiring. Jessa didn't think Mrs. Bailey's life was so bad. Living on a little farm with a few horses and a couple of cats seemed pretty reasonable.

Mrs. Bailey straightened up the jumble of spray bottles, bandages, and coffee mugs on the shelf by the phone. Her voice was a little rough when she spoke, as if she needed to clear her throat but couldn't.

"You think you've got problems. My brother died yesterday."

At first, Jessa thought Mrs. Bailey was joking. "You don't have a brother!" she said.

Mrs. Bailey's smile was tinged with something close to sadness. "Nope. Not any more."

Jessa's eyebrows pushed together.

"We were never close," Mrs. Bailey said brusquely. "I'm eighteen years younger than he is . . . was. We really never had much to say to each other." She restacked the coffee cups on the shelf.

Jessa couldn't think of a thing to say. It didn't seem appropriate to offer sympathy because Mrs. Bailey didn't really seem *that* upset. It was all very strange. Why was Mrs. Bailey bringing it up at all?

"Would you like some hot chocolate?" Jessa asked finally.

Mrs. Bailey nodded and sat down on her tack trunk.

"Pete was a funny old buzzard," she said. "He mostly kept to himself. He had a nice place in the Kootenays where he kept a few sheep and some chickens. Then, a couple of years ago, he bought a team of Belgians." ·

Mrs. Bailey sighed heavily.

"The old fool never did a thing with Harpo and Markus, as far as I know. I think he meant to enter them in pulling competitions, or something—but never got around to it."

Mrs. Bailey looked straight at Jessa.

"Well, you know where those two horses are winding up, don't you?"

Jessa's eyes widened. "Here?"

Mrs. Bailey nodded.

"But . . . where are we going to put them?" Dark Creek Stables was a small place. There were already five horses in residence. At a pinch, Mrs. Bailey had room for six if she moved the tractor out of the second stall in the original barn.

The main barn had four roomy box stalls. The older barn had two smaller stalls. Rebel spent his nights in one of those. The tractor lived in the other.

Jessa couldn't imagine where Mrs. Bailey was going to squeeze in two big draft horses.

"I guess we'll find room for them somewhere. We don't have much choice. A truck is bringing them over on the ferry on Saturday."

Mrs. Bailey sipped her hot chocolate.

"Mmmmm, that's just what I needed. Thank you, Jessa.

"Now, you'd better go and catch Rebel if you want to have time to ride before dark," she added curtly. "And then, you have to get home to do your homework. Not before you finish your chores, of course."

Jessa walked to Rebel's paddock thinking that the winter months lasted far too long. It got dark way too early and everything was always damp. To top it all off, Jessa's nose never seemed to stop running.

Rebel didn't look too happy, either. With his head down and his tail turned to the wind, he looked positively forlorn. When he spotted Jessa, he perked up, anxious to come in from the cold. He could hardly wait to get out of his paddock and he pushed past her as they navigated the frozen puddle at the gate. Jessa led him right into Brandy's box stall and tied him to the ring in the corner.

Earlier, Jessa had peeked into Billy Jack's stall. As usual, it was a mess. Mrs. Bailey always left his stall for Jessa to clean on the three days during the week she helped at the barn. Jessa did all the barn chores on the weekends. Most days she didn't mind the work. Her hours at the barn paid for Rebel's board. Without her contribution, Jessa's mother wouldn't be able to afford a horse at all. Whenever Jessa felt like complaining, she thought of all the things her mother couldn't buy because of horse expenses: a better car, a proper vacation.

Jessa quickly groomed Rebel, tacked him up, and led him out to the mounting block at the end of the barn. She still couldn't believe how lucky she was to be able to use the smart-looking bay pony. He was part quarter horse and part Welsh pony, quick and strong, and a great little jumper.

His real owner had several horses and no time to ride Rebel. Jessa paid for all his expenses in exchange for being the only one to ride him. It was the next best thing to actually owning a horse.

Jessa settled gently into the saddle. From her perch on Rebel's back she could just see the big field behind Mrs.

Bailey's house. Mrs. Bailey was putting in a riding ring back there. Out in the field the tractor stood idle.

It had probably broken down again. The ring was supposed to have been finished by now. At this rate, it would be next summer before she and Rebel could practise their flat-work properly without riding half an hour down the trail to the ring at the Arbutus Lane Equestrian Centre.

Jessa checked her girth and tightened the chinstrap on her helmet. Rebel's shoes crunched on the gravel of the long driveway.

When they turned onto the Dark Creek Railway Trail, Jessa eased Rebel into a trot. Before long, she could hardly move her fingers, and her toes felt as if they had frozen solid.

She sniffled in the cold and concentrated on her riding. Even though she was freezing, there was no reason not to ride properly.

Jessa had just dropped her stirrups and started a series of leg-yielding exercises, weaving back and forth across the trail, when Rebel raised his head, pricked up his ears, and let out a loud squealing whinny.

Up ahead, another rider raised his hand and waved. Even at a distance, Jessa knew right away who it was. She often ran into Jeremy Digsby out on the trail. He actually preferred to school his magnificent black Andalusian, Caspian, outside the confines of a riding ring.

Jeremy's mother, Rebecca, was one of Western Canada's best horse trainers. Jessa had heard a story that she had ridden until two days before Jeremy was born.

He sure rode as if he were born in the saddle. He wanted to be an international eventer, and there weren't many days when he stayed at home and didn't ride at all.

"Cold enough for you?" he asked when he drew alongside Jessa.

Caspian snorted and puffed steam from his nostrils. Jessa thought he looked like a noble steed from a fairy tale, especially when he arched his neck and pawed the ground.

She laughed and nodded. "Maybe this will be it for cold this year," she said.

"Somehow I doubt it," Jeremy replied.

The winters on southern Vancouver Island were usually the mildest in Canada. Some years, the city of Victoria didn't see any snow at all. Jessa hoped that was going to be the case this year. Keeping to her riding schedule all winter was the only way she and Rebel could stay competitive against the kids who kept their horses at the big barns with indoor riding rings.

"Are you going away for Christmas?" Jeremy asked.

Jessa shook her head. "Are you?"

"Unfortunately," he said. "We're visiting my uncle in California. I would rather stay here and ride."

"I know what you mean," Jessa agreed. She was looking forward to riding every day over the holidays.

"You'll have a good time," she said, trying to make light of his looming departure. It was hard to sound convincing. She had secretly hoped that at least *some* of her holiday rides would be with Jeremy and Caspian.

"At least California will be warmer than *this*," he said and pulled a face.

Rebel shifted impatiently and flipped his nose, pulling the reins through Jessa's fingers. It really was too cold to be standing around talking, even to a boy as nice as Jeremy.

"I guess we'd better go," he said. "It's going to get dark soon."

Rebel danced in place, anxious to be moving again.

"Have a good trip!" Jessa said as she gave her pony a squeeze with her legs.

Jeremy nodded and waved before trotting off along the

wide, level trail.

Jessa sniffled. She covered the tip of her nose with her glove and tried to warm it up with a puff of her breath. She clucked to Rebel and urged him into a brisk trot, then organized her reins, collected the trot, eased her left leg back, and asked for a canter.

Rebel's hooves drummed out a steady *ta-da-dum, ta-da-dum.* Jessa squinted. They weren't moving *that* fast, but the wind against her face stung her eyes with tears. It wasn't long before her toes ached from the cold. Her riding boots were too tight to wear with thick socks.

It seemed as if she and Rebel had only just started when it was time to turn around and head back to the barn. Jessa sure didn't want to be caught on the trail after dark.

Rebel walked along on a loose rein towards home. Jessa had a lot to do when she got back. Billy Jack's stall was waiting for her attention, and the horses would be more than ready for their evening feed. And a team of draft horses was coming! She decided she didn't even want to think about how long the chores would take once *they* arrived.

Jessa could understand why Mrs. Bailey was concerned about the newcomers. She vowed to try to do a little extra work around the barn so Mrs. Bailey wouldn't have quite so much to worry about. For one thing, the tack room needed a good cleanup. Maybe Cheryl would help her.

Rebel's head bobbed up and down with each relaxed stride he took, lulling Jessa into thoughts of completing dozens of projects at Dark Creek. If only school projects were so much fun! Jessa figured she'd be a straight A student.

3

"They're so huge!" Jessa gasped as she walked tentatively to where Mrs. Bailey stood with a lead shank in each hand. Mrs. Bailey looked as if she had shrunk three sizes.

Harpo and Markus towered over her, their massive shaggy heads raised to get a better look at their new surroundings. Jessa had been expecting a couple of big horses, but these two were giants.

"Which is which?" she asked.

"This one's Harpo," said Mrs. Bailey. "He's a little bigger." The taller horse had two white socks in front. Both were the colour of honey, with long, wild manes. Nearly identical white blazes splashed down their faces, narrowing as they reached the soft, pinkish muzzles.

"Where do you want us to unload all this other stuff?" asked the driver, gesturing into the back of the big truck that had just delivered the Belgians. His helper stood just inside the back of the truck, smoking. Jessa wrinkled her nose.

"Here! Hold them for a second, dear," said Mrs. Bailey, thrusting the two lead shanks at Jessa.

Reluctantly, Jessa took the horses from the older woman. What would happen if the giant pair decided to take off? Jessa didn't think she'd have much chance of stopping them.

"Whoa," she said as a preventive measure. Harpo lowered his head to get a better look at her. Ever so gently he stretched forward so he could sniff at her hair. His warm breath smelled vaguely of sweet, moist hay. Up close, Jessa could see Harpo's head was nearly twice as wide as Rebel's.

Mrs. Bailey disappeared into the gloom at the back of the truck. Jessa watched the horses as bumps and grunts emanated from somewhere up in front of where the horses had been tied. Even when Mrs. Bailey let out a low whistle of surprise, they stood quietly, their big ears swivelling slowly back and forth.

"There's a trunk full of harnesses and stuff," she said. "And a big wooden box or something under some old sleeping bags."

"You found the cutter, I guess," grinned the truck driver. "We had to take it apart to get it to fit back there."

"A cutter?" asked Jessa.

"What are we going to do with a horse-drawn sleigh here?" asked Mrs. Bailey of nobody in particular.

"It might snow," Jessa offered. "It's been pretty cold— I'm crossing my fingers for a white Christmas!" She began to sing. "Oh, what fun it is to ride on a two-horse open sleigh!"

Mrs. Bailey looked at Jessa and grinned. Harpo nodded his big head and Markus tentatively pawed at the gravel in the parking area.

"See! They'd love to pull a sleigh!" Jessa laughed.

The driver shook his head. "A sleigh has two sets of runners: front and back. A cutter just has one and it's shaped differently in the front. When we unload it, you'll see."

"Oh," said Jessa. "On a two-horse open cutter . . ."

The Christmas carol didn't have quite the same ring to it with the new lyrics.

The two men disappeared into the back of the truck to finish unloading.

"Let's put the horses in the big field up behind the house so I can keep an eye on them," Mrs. Bailey said as she took Harpo's lead rope from Jessa. "You can put the trunk and the cutter in the shavings shed," she called to the driver.

Harpo looked over his shoulder to make sure Markus and Jessa were right behind him and then quietly followed Mrs. Bailey up the driveway past the house. Mrs. Bailey liked to tell the story of how, years ago, she and her husband had cut down the trees to build their little log house.

The procession made its way through the gate into the big field.

Jessa walked beside Markus, a little afraid of his huge, hairy feet. His fetlocks were long and thick and the colour of pale yellow cream. Neither of the two arrivals had seen clippers for a long time.

Even though the big horse seemed to be only strolling along, Jessa had to move briskly to keep up with his long, easy stride. His great, gentle head bobbed up and down slightly with each step.

Jessa led him through the gate, and she and Mrs. Bailey slipped off the halters and watched the two new horses walk side by side up the small hill in the back field.

"Do you think they like doing everything together?" Jessa asked.

"Well, they are a team, aren't they?" said Mrs. Bailey. "I guess one would be lonely without the other," she added quietly. Jessa wondered if she was thinking about her brother.

Mrs. Bailey cleared her throat. "I suppose they'll find their hay before long." She turned away from the field. "Come on," she said to Jessa, who was lingering by the fence. "We'd better haul a couple more buckets of water for them. They're bound to be thirsty after their trip."

The outside pipes had frozen two nights in a row and still hadn't thawed out. Jessa's arms felt as if they had stretched to her knees from carrying heavy buckets of water from the house to the horse paddocks.

"Are you leaving them out all night?" Jessa asked.

"We don't have enough stalls in the barns," said Mrs. Bailey. "If it starts raining again they can shelter in the lean-to."

The lean-to was a three-sided wooden shelter at the far end of the field. It was just big enough for the two horses to stand in.

"They'll be fine," she said, seeing the worried look on Jessa's face. "Look at their winter coats. It's much colder in the Kootenays than it is here."

It was true. Harpo and Markus were certainly shaggy.

"Are you going away this Christmas?" Mrs. Bailey asked suddenly.

Jessa shook her head. "Are you?"

"I've decided to go away for a week with Betty. Warm these old bones of mine down south."

Betty King kept her pinto gelding, Brandy, at Dark Creek. She and Mrs. Bailey had been friends forever.

"Who will look after the horses?" Jessa asked slowly.

Mrs. Bailey smiled. "Do you think you can manage?"

Jessa swallowed hard. Mrs. Bailey never really had a break from looking after the horses. Even though Jessa did a good job of helping with the chores after school and on weekends, it wasn't nearly the same as taking on the responsibility of looking after everything at Dark Creek Stables.

Mrs. Bailey smiled at Jessa. "Don't look so worried! They're no trouble at all."

Jessa looked up at Mrs. Bailey with surprise. No trouble? That didn't sound like the Mrs. Bailey Jessa knew. Usually she had a list of dos and don'ts and be carefuls a mile long when it came to looking after the horses.

"But . . ." Jessa started.

Mrs. Bailey gave her a lopsided grin. She didn't like to smile because she said her teeth gave away her real age.

"Marjorie isn't going away, either. She'll be around to keep an eye on things. In fact, she's going to stay right here at the house while I'm gone. That way, she can feed Eric and Ariel, too."

Eric and Ariel were Mrs. Bailey's two rather rotund house cats. Mrs. Bailey often said it was a good thing they didn't live down in the barn because they were so lazy they would soon starve to death if they had to count on catching mice for dinner.

Jessa heaved a huge sigh of relief. Like all the women who kept their horses at Dark Creek, Marjorie Hamilton had been riding a long time. If she was going to be in charge, nothing too serious could go wrong.

"Sure, I'll help look after things here. Don't worry about a thing."

It was a lot easier to sound confident now that she knew Marjorie was going to be right up at the house while Mrs. Bailey was away.

"So, where are you and Betty going?"

Mrs. Bailey's eyes sparkled and for just a moment, she looked a little less tired. "Mexico. I sure wish we were leaving tomorrow."

4

"Jessa?"

Jessa dropped her bookbag on the kitchen floor and opened the fridge.

"Hi, Mom!" She poured herself a glass of milk and climbed on the counter to reach the can of chocolate milk powder.

Jessa fished a teaspoon out of the drawer and took her milk and the chocolate powder into the dining room to join her mother.

"Sit down." Her mother sounded serious, but not angry. Jessa couldn't think of why she might be in trouble. She hadn't chewed gum in the house for ages and she had remembered to clean the toilet without being asked.

"Your father phoned."

Jessa dug her spoon deep into the soft chocolate powder. Her father *never* phoned.

She tipped the mound of powder into her milk and tapped the spoon gently on the rim, then looked at her mother and asked, "Is he sick or something?"

Jessa could hardly remember her father. He had moved

to Japan about a year after he and her mother had split up. He barely ever wrote or called, though he usually remembered to send a card for Jessa's birthday. About two years after he moved to Tokyo he had married a Japanese woman, and last year, they had had a baby. Even though she told herself she didn't care if she ever saw him again, Jessa didn't think it would be a good thing if he was dying or something.

Jessa's mother shook her head and pushed a strand of hair behind her ear. Her eyes were dark and sad when she said, "He wants to come here to visit in December."

Jessa added another heaping spoonful of chocolate powder and stirred noisily, clinking her spoon against the side of her glass. Usually her mother asked her to stop after about ten clinks. Now, though, she said nothing as she waited for Jessa to speak.

Jessa loaded up another spoonful of powder. Her drink was a pleasant pale brown, but still far too milky for her taste.

"Why?" Jessa asked finally. "Why is he coming?"

"Well," her mother started, "I guess maybe he'd like to see you."

It seemed more than a little strange to Jessa that her father suddenly wanted to spend quality time with her. She stirred vigorously, whipping the milk up from the bottom of the glass until little chocolatey bubbles started forming on the top. She reached for another spoonful of powder.

"Don't you think you've got enough in there?" her mother asked.

"Just a couple more," Jessa said and quickly loaded up her spoon again.

"Did Granny tell him to come?"

"Not exactly. Several people from his company are

coming over to meet with some music producers in California. He was invited along on the trip because he speaks English and Japanese fluently."

"Oh." Jessa refused to be impressed.

"He's stopping here on his way back to Japan because . . . well, he got a very cheap airline ticket that allows him to take a side trip on the way. He was going to go to Las Vegas but your grandmother suggested it might be a good idea to stop by Victoria."

Jessa didn't know why she felt disappointed. She knew better than to expect much attention from her father. Maybe it was the thought of Christmas coming that had made her hope perhaps he was finally going to come for a visit.

Granny Richardson didn't think much of her son leaving his family in Canada, but she tried not to get too involved. Jessa did see her grandmother sometimes. Granny lived in Vancouver. When she made the ferry trip to Victoria, she and Jessa usually went to see a movie. If the weather was nice, they had ice cream cones in Beacon Hill Park. They almost never talked about her dad.

"How long is he staying here?" Jessa asked.

"Three days."

"Oh, great. At least we won't get tired of him," Jessa remarked dryly. She added two more spoonfuls of chocolate powder.

Her mother watched Jessa stir the thick, chocolatey drink. "Jessa, please try to be nice."

"Where's he going to sleep?"

"I thought you could sleep in my room with me and he could stay up in yours."

"What!? In my room?"

"Jessa, where else could he sleep?"

"What's wrong with the couch?"

"Jessa, please. Be reasonable. It's only for three days."

Jessa skimmed a teaspoonful of little bubbles from the top of her milk and dribbled them slowly off the end of her teaspoon onto the tip of her tongue. She pressed some undissolved powder granules against the back of her front teeth with the tip of her tongue. The soft lumps melted into the sweet taste of chocolate. She added more powder to the glass.

"So, when does he get here?"

"December twenty-first. He's leaving on Christmas Eve."

"I guess he has to get home to his *real* family for Christmas." Jessa sighed. She thought her father was very inconsiderate to disrupt her holidays like this, especially if he was going to stay in her room up in the eaves of their little house.

"Are you two going to argue?"

Jessa's mother shook her head.

"He left a long, long time ago, Jessa. It was the best thing for all of us. He wasn't happy here, and I certainly didn't want to move to Japan."

Jessa had heard the story before, but it still didn't make much sense to her. How could someone be in love and get married and then just suddenly decide to move to a foreign country?

Her mother's various attempts at explaining everything hadn't really been too successful. Jessa found it all very confusing.

Most of the time, she just didn't think about it. Except now, he was about to show up, invade her room, and ruin her Christmas. How was she supposed to ignore *that*?

"Your dad is coming at Christmas?" Monika asked.

"I thought you said you didn't know who your dad

was?" Sarah interjected.

"You told me he was dead," said Rachel.

Jessa carved a thin wedge from the side of her piece of turkey. In honour of Christmas, the school cafeteria had served turkey-flavoured meals all week. Jessa didn't like talking about her father. Sometimes she told people she didn't know where he was. It was embarrassing that he rarely wrote and never came to visit.

"Dead? That's just a metaphor for living in Japan," Cheryl said, trying to come to Jessa's rescue. "He's a spy, you know."

"He is *not*," Jessa sputtered. She and Cheryl liked to make up stories about her dad, but they weren't meant to be shared around the cafeteria.

"He works with satellites and radios," Jessa said. In truth, she wasn't totally sure *what* he did for a living. Maybe he *was* a spy.

Sarah, Rachel, and the other girls at the table didn't seem to be that interested in hearing about Jessa's father, spy or not.

"We leave tomorrow night for Whistler," said Sarah. "I already know I'm getting a new snowboard for Christmas. I can't wait to get to the mountains."

Sarah was tall and slender. She wore a new pair of black and teal snowboarding pants and a warm purple sweater.

"Are you going anywhere, Rachel?" Cheryl asked. Jessa fully expected Rachel to launch into a long description of some fancy holiday—a snorkelling trip in Barbados, or a cruise in the Mediterranean.

But Rachel shook her head. "Dad won't be back from New York until the weekend. We've got two new mares arriving from Arizona. I guess we'll be getting them settled in."

Jessa's stomach lurched. Sometimes she was so jealous

of Rachel's dream life she could hardly stand to be in the same room with her. She wondered if the day would ever come when she and Rachel could be friends.

"We've got two new horses at Dark Creek," she said, and immediately wished she hadn't opened her mouth. Rachel was talking about purebred Arabians, some of the finest horses in the world. Jessa was thinking of two clunky old draft horses with no value to anyone.

Rachel completely ignored Jessa. "This one mare we're getting is from really old Polish bloodlines, and Dad says that I can have her first foal if I help around the place and learn more about the breeding side of the business."

Jessa pushed her plate away and slumped back into her chair in disgust. She wondered if there was a cure for jealousy. Probably no more likely than there was a cure for rude snobbery.

Rachel had a perfectly nice Arabian mare called Gazelle. She was the last person on the planet who needed *another* horse.

"Right, Jessa?" Cheryl asked.

"What?" Jessa had completely missed what her friend had said. She hoped the lunch hour would end soon. She had promised her mother she would take advantage of the last few lunch hours before Christmas break to work on her journal assignment.

So far, she had managed to avoid actually doing any work at all on the project. The closest she had come was a long discussion about corsets with Cheryl.

"Jessa, you're not paying attention. What *are* you thinking about?"

"Corsets, if you must know," Jessa snapped.

Rachel snorted and covered her mouth with a table napkin. Her eyes bulged and then she swallowed her mouthful of milk.

"Can you imagine if we had to wear corsets?" Sarah asked.

"Not that you'd ever need one," Cheryl quipped.

"My mom's friend says you can't ever be too thin or too rich," said Rachel, who had recovered her composure.

"My brother's girlfriend, Bernie, said that tight pants are just as bad as corsets," Cheryl added.

"What do you mean?" Rachel asked.

"She said they've discovered a new disease you get when you wear pants that are too tight."

"Yeah, right," said Sarah.

"You don't have to worry in *those*," Cheryl said, pointing at Sarah's baggy snowboarding pants. "Seriously, Bernie saw a documentary about people who wear pants so tight they squish their intestines. Then they can't digest properly and they get terrible . . ." Cheryl paused for dramatic effect. ". . . flatulence." She bulged her eyes out and pinched her lips together.

"Terrible what?" Rachel asked.

"Gasssssss . . ."

Jessa giggled. Bernie was a great source of interesting information. PBS was her favourite television station.

5

Mrs. Bailey kicked at the fallen gatepost with the wet toe of her green Wellington boot.

"I should just sell the place!" she said. Jessa and Mrs. Bailey stood side by side in the icy drizzle. "Just look at what they've done!"

Jessa stared in horror at the gatepost in Harpo and Markus's field. Instead of standing up supporting the metal farm gate, the fat post was lying down in a muddy puddle.

The gate itself was off its hinges and had a distinct buckle through the middle. Both ends lifted slightly off the muddy ground.

Jessa shivered in the cold. A gust of wind blew sharp prickles of rain against her cheeks. "Maybe the two of us could straighten up the post," she offered.

"Look at the darn thing a little closer, Jessa," snorted Mrs. Bailey.

Jessa sloshed forward and leaned over to inspect the post more carefully. It wasn't just leaning over, it was snapped right off at the bottom. The whole thing would have to be replaced!

Jessa peered along the fenceline. Three rails had pulled off when the post had come down. All along the edge of the field, posts leaned out slightly, and in several places, cross-rails had snapped in the middle.

The fence looked not only wiggly but rather insecure, too. There was a lot of work to be done to make the field horse-proof again.

"What have they been doing in here?" Jessa asked.

Mrs. Bailey shook her head. "That Harpo keeps sticking his darn head out between the rails. Then he leans forward to eat the grass on the outside. The rails just can't handle it! I counted eight rails down."

"What about all those posts?" Jessa asked.

Mrs. Bailey looked disgusted. "Markus. That horse has the itchiest hind end I've ever seen! He backs up to a post and scratches against it for ages! I watched him from the kitchen window the other morning. When he was done scratching one side of his back end, he turned around and backed up again to scratch the other side. Then, when he was finished, he strolled over to another fence post and started all over again!"

Jessa couldn't help smiling. No wonder the fence posts were keeling over, with Markus sitting on them!

"I tell you, Jessa, it's just not worth it! I can't keep up any more. Look at the tractor, too! It's *still* out in the middle of the field."

Jessa followed Mrs. Bailey's gesture and looked at the blue lump sitting in the middle of the soggy field. Mrs. Bailey had covered the old tractor with a huge blue tarpaulin. Jessa wondered if the tractor would ever start again.

"I'm just going to put the place on the market and be done with it. Then I could move into a little apartment in town where I wouldn't even have a lawn to mow."

"We can all help," Jessa said, thinking she would call the other boarders. "We could have a fence-mending party."

"Hmph," said Mrs. Bailey. "Let's get out of the cold and figure out where to put those troublemakers."

Jessa followed Mrs. Bailey back to the barn. It had already rained steadily for two days and the forecast wasn't offering any relief.

The driveway and barnyard were a sea of mud. Water poured from the broken gutter at the end of the barn. The downpipe had snapped off in the summer when Jessa had cut the corner too close as she was leaving with Rebel for a trail ride. The toe of her riding boot had caught the pipe and Rebel had spooked sideways. The whole drainpipe had clattered to the ground, sending Rebel prancing all the way to the end of the driveway.

Jessa wished now she had made a point of fixing it instead of just moving the pipe out of the way.

Harpo and Markus raised their big shaggy heads where they stood in the cross-ties as Jessa and Mrs. Bailey ducked out of the rain and into the covered walkway.

The other horses poked their heads over their stall doors, trying to make friends with the two newcomers who were tied tantalizingly just out of reach.

Harpo pushed his big, soft nose into the bend of Jessa's elbow and gave her a gentle nudge. His long, unkempt forelock fell over his eyes. Jessa reached up and gave him a scratch behind the ears. As if he knew what a stretch it was for her to reach, he lowered his head and held very still.

"Where are you going to keep them now?" she asked.

Mrs. Bailey shook her head. "They're inseparable. About the only place we have is the old barn."

Jessa looked horrified. The old barn had only two stalls. The tractor usually lived in one of them. The other was Rebel's.

Across the stable-yard, she could just see Rebel's black nose poking out over his stall door. After a moment, he pulled his head back into the dark warmth of his stall and disappeared from view.

Jessa had to admit it did make sense to put Harpo and Markus in the old barn. They could be together, and even though it didn't look like much, the old building was solid. The original owner of Dark Creek had built it out of railway ties. Jessa figured the building was virtually indestructible.

"But what about Rebel?" she asked. Mrs. Bailey didn't answer her right away. Jasmine nickered softly, and Mrs. Bailey went to her stall door.

"Candy?" she murmured. Mrs. Bailey slipped her horse a Fisherman's Friend cough drop. Jessa didn't know how Jasmine could stand the strongly flavoured morsels, but the big chestnut mare loved them. It was impossible not to laugh at the noisy slurping sounds she made as she sucked away at the little treat. Still stroking Jasmine's neck, Mrs. Bailey turned back to Jessa.

"Someone will have to take the paddock by the driveway, the one with the best shelter. We could bed it deeply and put some plywood up on the open side," she said. "It's not perfect, but it would do until I can sell these two and get the little barn back. I really have no use for them—and definitely no room."

Jessa looked at the two golden Belgians, still damp from the rain. During the time they had spent in the big field, they had completely ignored the available shelter.

There was no doubt in her mind that when Mrs. Bailey said "someone" would have to take the front paddock, she was thinking of Rebel. Jessa knew that Marjorie would never let Babe sleep anywhere less than the best. It hardly seemed fair that Mrs. Bailey would have to put her beloved Jasmine in second-rate accommodations.

Even though Brandy and Billy Jack were easily tough enough to handle paddock life for a while, Jessa doubted their owners could. Sharon Davies and Betty King were both getting older and neither of them was quite as hardy as Mrs. Bailey. They didn't ride much when the weather was awful, but they both came down to the barn several times a week to groom their horses and visit with Mrs. Bailey.

Jessa sighed. "I'll go tell Rebel he's moving," she said. "I'll meet you in the tack room in a few minutes." She hunched up her shoulders and pulled her coat close around her before splashing across the yard to visit her horse and break the bad news.

6

Jessa and Cheryl hardly talked to each other all week. Jessa finally phoned her friend to ask her if she'd like to help paint the tack room.

"I guess so."

"After we've finished painting, maybe you could give me some suggestions about my socials project."

Cheryl sucked in a breath on the other end of the line. "Actually, I'm doing my journal project with Monika."

Neither girl spoke, and Jessa found herself wishing she hadn't asked Cheryl to come to the barn.

"So, when do you want to meet up?" Cheryl asked.

"Early, I guess. So we can get the painting over with."

"Eight o'clock early enough?"

Jessa sighed. She hated getting up early. "Fine. I'll see you at the barn." She hung up the phone and leaned against the kitchen wall. The idea of sprucing up the barn for Mrs. Bailey didn't seem quite as exciting any more.

By 8:15 the next morning, the girls had already moved all the saddles out of the tack room.

"How can you possibly remember which is which?"

Cheryl asked, holding two bridles in front of her. She stood halfway up the ladder leading to the hayloft.

"It's obvious," Jessa said, looking down at her friend through the trap door at the top. "This one's Jasmine's," she said, reaching down and taking one of the bridles from Cheryl. "It would be way too big for Babe. And do you think anyone else would be caught dead wearing any of Billy Jack's western stuff?"

Cheryl shrugged and turned around to climb back down the ladder to get more tack to pass up to Jessa.

When everything was finally moved, Jessa and Cheryl stood in the middle of the little room. Without any tack it looked very tidy.

"What about the tack trunks?" Cheryl asked.

"We'll cover them up. That's why I brought the old sheets."

Jessa fished a couple of flowery sheets from a plastic shopping bag.

"Are you sure your mother won't mind?" Cheryl asked.

"We can wash them," Jessa said. "See—water soluble. It says so right on the can." She nudged at the paint can with her rubber boot. "Mom will never know. Besides, they're old. We never use them anyway."

Cheryl helped Jessa cover the two big tack trunks with the sheets.

"I sure hope Mrs. Bailey likes what we're doing," said Cheryl.

"Of course she will," said Jessa. "Here—start painting."

Jessa put a wide, flat paintbrush into Cheryl's hand. She knelt down and pried the lid of the paint can off with a screwdriver she had brought from home.

"I'm impressed," Cheryl said, dipping her brush into the can. "You thought of everything."

"Look at this," Jessa said, pulling a sign from her bag.

DO NOT ENTER!
MAJOR CLEAN-UP IN PROGRESS!

She taped the sign to the outside of the tack room door with a roll of tape she also pulled from her bag.

Jessa concentrated on not dripping paint on the floor as she climbed up onto one of the covered tack trunks. It was hard to work in the same room with Cheryl and not talk about school.

Carefully, she painted the wall around all the bridle hooks.

"If we do a project like this every weekend, Mrs. Bailey will see how easy it is to keep the place looking great. When we get a dry day, we can paint the fence along the driveway."

Jessa was surprised at how quickly she and Cheryl finished painting the little tack room. When they were done, they sat side by side to survey their work.

"Where is Mrs. Bailey, anyway?" Cheryl asked.

"She has a bad cold. She's up at the house," Jessa said.

"When can we bring the saddles and stuff back down?" Cheryl asked.

Jessa looked doubtfully at every surface in the small room. There wasn't a single paint-free place to put anything. She shrugged her shoulders and looked around for a felt pen to write a new sign warning everyone about the wet paint. Just then the phone rang.

Both girls jumped and looked at each other. The phone rang again. It seemed loud and insistent in the quiet little room.

"Maybe Mrs. Bailey unplugged the phone in the house so she could sleep," Cheryl suggested.

"What if it's my mom?" Jessa asked.

The phone rang again and Jessa walked over and stood in front of it.

"Should I answer it?" she asked.

Another ring.

"What should I do?"

"It must be important or the person would have given up by now," said Cheryl.

"I'm not supposed to answer the phone."

Jessa slowly reached forward, hoping the phone would stop ringing. But it didn't stop. Hardly realizing what she was doing, she felt the cool hard receiver in her hand on the next ring.

She took a breath to say "Hello, Dark Creek" when she heard Mrs. Bailey's voice on the house extension.

"Hello?" Mrs. Bailey sounded very sick.

"Hello! Roslyn Anderson here. High-Ho Carriage Co.—returning your call."

The woman's voice on the other end of the line was loud and cheerful.

Jessa put her hand over the mouthpiece. She didn't dare hang the phone up again or Mrs. Bailey would hear a click and know she had picked up the phone in the barn.

Her heart pounded. She didn't know what to do with the phone. There was nowhere to put it down because everything was still covered with fresh wet paint. She hoped desperately she wouldn't drop the receiver or have a sneezing fit or anything.

She gripped the phone, still not believing she was listening in on someone else's conversation.

"I called to find out if you might be interested in buying a pair of Belgians," Mrs. Bailey was saying.

The High-Ho Carriage Company gave carriage tours to tourists who visited Victoria. Their horse-drawn vehicles looked sort of like streetcars and were pulled by teams of draft horses.

"Actually, we're over-horsed at the moment," Roslyn

said. "I'm bringing along two new teams this winter. We're pretty crowded out at the farm at the best of times."

Mrs. Bailey coughed and sighed. "I see. Well, do you have any idea who might be interested in buying a couple of draft horses?"

"Not really. There's a draft horse club up-island. You might try calling someone up there. Have you tried an ad in the *Colonialist?* Or in one of the horse classified magazines?"

"No. Not yet," admitted Mrs. Bailey. "I'd sure like to find a good home for them. I guess the ads are my next move."

"Good luck!" Roslyn said.

After Mrs. Bailey hung up, Jessa quickly and quietly slipped the receiver back into the cradle.

"What was that all about?" Cheryl whispered. She had been beside herself with curiosity while Jessa was listening to the conversation.

"Mrs. Bailey is trying to sell Harpo and Markus," Jessa whispered back.

"Why are we whispering?" Cheryl asked.

Jessa shrugged. She wondered what would happen if Mrs. Bailey couldn't find a buyer for the two newcomers. Despite the extra work they created, Jessa kind of liked having the two friendly giants around.

7

"You do realize I shouldn't be helping you?"

"Yeah, yeah, I know. Come on, let's find your brother."

Jessa and Cheryl hung up their rain slickers in the front hallway of Cheryl's house. Loud music blared from the living room.

Cheryl's brother, Anthony, had books about everything on his shelves.

"Let's see if he's in here," Cheryl said, blowing a huge purple bubble-gum bubble. The music was so loud, Jessa could hardly hear what her friend was saying.

Cheryl pushed the living room door open and immediately pulled it shut again. She grabbed Jessa's wrist and dragged her halfway up the stairs.

"What are you doing?"

"Shh! Shh! They'll hear us!"

"Who?"

"Oh, yuck! I can't believe it!"

"What? Who's in the living room?"

Cheryl rolled her eyes. "Bernie was sitting on Anthony's lap!"

"So? That's what boyfriends and girlfriends *do*."

"No, it's worse than that. She was smearing something sticky on his head!"

"Oh, gross! That's disgusting! What do you think they're doing?"

"I do not care to know," said Cheryl primly.

"*Now* what are we going to do?" Jessa asked.

Cheryl extended her hand gracefully, indicating Jessa was supposed to continue up the stairs.

"But—"

"If Anthony wishes to misbehave with Miss Bernadette, then we shall have to take matters into our own hands."

"We can't just go into his room without asking!"

"Look, Jessa. Do you want to find a book for your homework or not?"

Jessa looked doubtful.

"He's let us go in there before. He won't mind."

Cheryl climbed to the top of the stairs. Jessa didn't have much choice but to follow.

The two girls stood outside Anthony's bedroom door.

"What if they come up?"

"They won't, believe me. Bernie looked very interested in whatever she was doing to Anthony."

With a determined nod, Cheryl pushed the door open.

"Anthony!" she gasped in horror.

"Well, whom did you expect? This *is* my room. Nice of you to knock!"

"I . . . oh . . . oh, Anthony . . ." Cheryl stood in the doorway with her mouth hanging open.

Jessa looked back towards the stairs. She could still hear music from the living room. If Anthony was up in his room, then who was downstairs with Bernie?

She and Cheryl looked at each other in utter horror.

"Jeez," said Anthony, looking past the girls. "She really

has that music cranked up." He got up and brushed past them.

"No!" squealed Cheryl. "Don't go down there!"

"Why not?"

"Errr . . . we have a very important, very difficult home-work assignment and we really, really need your help."

Anthony ran his hand through his curly red hair. You could see from a mile away that he and Cheryl were related.

"You know where the books are. Help yourselves."

He strode down the hall and disappeared down the stairs.

Jessa and Cheryl stood frozen. Jessa's heart fluttered wildly. She chewed her gum nervously and blew a quick bubble. Cheryl jumped when it snapped.

Timidly, the two girls sat down in Anthony's room. The last thing they could imagine doing was looking through all his books. They strained to hear what was happening downstairs. Suddenly the music stopped.

"Wait! Where are you going?"

But Cheryl was gone. Jessa caught up with her on the stairs.

Both girls leaned forward as far as they could but they couldn't quite see what was going on in the living room.

"Bernie! What are you doing! Look at that ugly face!" they heard Anthony say.

Jessa and Cheryl exchanged horrified looks.

"Let me rearrange it for you!"

"No!" shrieked Cheryl, tearing into the living room. Jessa was right behind her. She fully expected Anthony to be attacking Bernadette's new boyfriend.

Jessa ran right into Cheryl who had stopped dead in the middle of the room.

"Hi, girls," Bernie said cheerfully. She was holding a bowl full of carrot-coloured goop in one hand.

"What do you think? He's almost finished."

Jessa and Cheryl stared at Bernie's latest creation—a chair sculpted in the shape of a life-sized man. He was dressed in a pair of Anthony's black pants and had Anthony's trademark red scarf draped around his neck.

Bernie sat back down on the chair's lap and smeared a bit more orange paste on its head.

"Anthony, come over here a second so I can get this hairline right."

"He's very . . . realistic," Jessa said politely.

"What are you girls studying?" Bernie asked, smudging a bit of brown paint onto her sculpture's temple with her thumb.

Cheryl explained the homework assignment.

"I have some ancient history books up there," Anthony said. "Greeks and Romans. But no Victorian-era stuff."

Jessa was hardly surprised. So far, nothing about this assignment had been easy.

"Do you girls keep journals?" Bernie asked.

"Of course I do!" Cheryl said.

Jessa kept quiet. Nothing interesting ever happened to *her*. Certainly nothing worth writing about.

Bernie studied Anthony's curly hair. She picked up a toothpick and drew squiggly lines in the orange goop on the chair's head.

"When you keep a journal, you're writing history as it happens," she said. "I keep a journal. When I'm famous, my biographers will thank me."

Looking at Bernie's chair-man with his crooked nose and sunken eyes, Jessa couldn't quite believe she was really in the presence of a great artist. Just to be safe, she decided to hang on to the pencil drawings Bernie had done of Rebel at the end of the summer. They might just be worth something one day.

8

December 20
Dear Diary,
Tomorrow is the last day of school before the holidays. I can't wait! Here is my list of things to do with Rebel.

    1. leg-yielding
    2. counter-canter
    3. ask Mrs. B. about hunt clip

    My dad arrives tomorrow at 5:10 PM. Yuck. At least he's not staying for Christmas.

Jessa slipped her new diary inside a bigger book about horse grooming. Her mother thought she was doing her homework. This diary business was a nuisance. How could Cheryl and Bernie think it was so great?

She flopped down on her bed and stared up at the poster of a Lipizzaner stallion she had stuck on her ceiling. The rearing horse looked like a piece of marble sculpture.

It was hard not to think about Cheryl and Monika. All week they had been practising their journal play together.

Right at that very moment they were over at Cheryl's house trying on costumes.

Jessa got up and pulled her diary from its hiding place. She added a sentence to the end of her entry.

I need a new best friend.

"Jessa! You're so grown up!" Her father sat opposite her at a corner booth in Whitey's Family Restaurant. "You look just like your mother."

This guy's original, Jessa thought and then caught herself. What was he supposed to say to a virtual stranger? He had been nice enough to offer to take her and her mom out for dinner on their way home from the airport.

Even though he was obviously trying to find something to say to her, Jessa didn't feel like easing his awkwardness by making light conversation.

"So, what's with this cold weather?" he asked.

Jessa was tired of thinking about the weather. The rain and cold made barn chores really unpleasant.

Mrs. Bailey had the right idea. Her flight to Acapulco was scheduled to leave on December twenty-seventh. Jessa wasn't looking forward to all the extra work she'd have to do while Mrs. Bailey and Betty were away.

"When we were flying into Victoria, the pilot said it might actually snow in time for Christmas. Looks like I picked a good year for a visit, don't you think?"

Jessa nodded. It seemed rude not to give him even that much acknowledgement.

Jessa's mother sat down at the table. "I heard two women in the washroom talking about the weather," she said. "One of them said it might snow as early as tomorrow."

"Great!" Jessa said, deliberately not looking at her father. "A white Christmas would be excellent!"

Her parents exchanged awkward glances. It was really strange to see them sitting together at the restaurant table.

Jessa felt a pang of jealousy. What if she wanted to talk to her mother privately about something? Now she'd have to find a moment when the two of them would be alone.

Then Jessa had a horrifying thought. What if her father and mother fell in love all over again? It *had* happened once before. Then what?

Would he move back into the house? Would Jessa have to give up her room permanently? Jessa felt quite ill as she realized that if her parents got back together, her father wouldn't be sleeping in Jessa's room.

For the first time since his arrival, Jessa studied her father. He was sort of good-looking with his sandy-coloured hair and friendly blue eyes. Even though he must have been terribly nervous, he didn't really show it. He looked quite happy, Jessa thought.

He smiled across the table at her and Jessa blushed. She forced her thoughts away and, without saying "thank you," grabbed the mug of hot chocolate the waitress brought to the table. It was pale and watery-looking compared to the thick brew she liked to make at home.

"Jessa! Manners!" her mother said sharply.

Jessa took a big gulp of hot chocolate and immediately wished she hadn't. In her haste she had burned her tongue. Her eyes watered and she clamped her teeth together trying to ignore the way her tongue felt flat and sort of scaly.

She decided her father's visit had already lasted too long.

"Can you drop me off at the barn on the way home?" she asked.

"Jessa!" Her mother shot her a disapproving look.

"I won't be long. I know it's dark. You could pick me up at 8:30," Jessa wheedled.

"It's okay, Susan," her father interrupted quickly. "I'm really tired. I could do with a nap."

Jessa groaned inwardly as she thought of their house guest settling himself into her bed. She was glad she had suggested going to the barn. At least he wasn't likely to follow her down there. Besides, Rebel's tack needed a good cleaning. While she was at it, she could do Jasmine's, too.

9

Early the next morning Jessa slipped out of the house before her mother could make other plans. It was the first day of the holidays, and Jessa intended to spend it doing exactly what she wanted.

It wasn't hard to find things to keep her occupied down at the barn. Under a threatening sky, she and Rebel enjoyed a quick ride along the trail that led past the golf course. "Your mane sure looks good," she said, admiring the pulling job she had done.

By the time Jessa had scrubbed the water buckets and arranged all the items on the tack room shelf by size, Mrs. Bailey was beginning to think she would never go home again.

"Jessa, you'd better leave before it gets too dark to ride your bike."

"Okay."

When she finally arrived home shortly before dinner-time, her father was just waking up on the couch.

"He insisted on moving into the living room," her mother said quietly as she peeled potatoes in the kitchen.

"He didn't think it was fair you should have to give up your bedroom for him. He finally gave up waiting for you to come home. A couple of hours ago he decided to have a nap."

Jessa felt strangely guilty. She decided it wouldn't kill her to be a little nicer to him.

"Jessa?"

"What?"

"Do you know why there's paint all over my spare sheets?"

Jessa stared at the floor. "I thought it would come out. I washed them twice."

Her mother changed the subject when Jessa's father walked into the kitchen to join them. "It's starting to snow," she said.

"Really?" He peered out through the kitchen window. In the glow of the nearby street lamp, the swirling flakes glistened against the wintry darkness of the evening sky.

Jessa's mother gave her a look that promised Jessa hadn't heard the end of the sheets.

"Hey!" he said suddenly. "Do you still have our skis?"

Jessa's mother plopped the last of the potatoes into the pot of boiling water. "You know," she said, "they may still be down in the basement. I'll look after dinner."

"I didn't know you had skis," Jessa said, a little put out. Jessa rarely went down into the basement. It smelled like rotten mushrooms, the stairs creaked as if they were about to collapse, and there were big, dark brown spiders everywhere.

"Cross-country skis," her mother said. "Remember that trip we made when I was pregnant?"

Jessa's parents laughed.

"I sure wish I'd had a camera," her father said. "Remember when you tipped over and fell into the snowbank? You were so round you couldn't get up again!"

Her mother chuckled. "I remember you were laughing so hard you couldn't help me up."

Jessa left the kitchen and started climbing up the narrow stairs that led to her bedroom under the eaves.

"Jessa?"

"I'm going to work on my socials project," Jessa said, figuring her mother would never argue with that.

At least she had a room to go to, she thought as she trudged heavily up the stairs.

Jessa plopped down on her bed. Beside her lay four history books. She ignored them and retrieved her diary.

December 22
Only three days until Christmas! My dad got here yesterday. So far I am ignoring him.

Jessa wanted to write something about Cheryl, but all she could think of was wishing they were best friends again. And *that* reminded her they still weren't getting along too well.

There was a soft knock at the door. Her mother opened it and handed her the portable phone.

"Don't talk too long, dinner's almost ready."

It was Cheryl.

"Jessa, you're in *big* trouble."

"What are you talking about?"

"Remember when you were chewing gum in Anthony's room?"

"Yeah. Why am I in trouble?"

"Well, Bernie and Anthony were doing some yoga thing in his room—"

"Yoga thing?" Jessa interrupted.

54

"Bernie thinks standing on her head helps her creative juices flow."

"What does that have to do with me?" Jessa asked.

"Bernie had just finished an upside-down insect position and she went to scratch her head and guess what was stuck in her hair?"

"What?"

"Your gum!"

"*My* gum?!"

"Well, *you* were the one who sat on the floor," Cheryl pointed out.

"So did you."

"No. I sat on the bed, far from the place the gum was found."

"I didn't leave my gum lying around!" Surely Cheryl was joking!

"Thanks to you, we're not allowed to go in Anthony's room any more."

"It was probably *your* gum!"

"It doesn't matter," Cheryl said grumpily. "Bernie said it really hurt to try and pull it out. She's pretty mad at you. Anthony says she has a little bald patch now."

"How could you blame something like that on me? You're the one who's always chewing gum."

"I don't want to talk about this any more," Cheryl said.

"Neither do I."

There was a long, stony silence when neither girl said anything.

"I guess I should get back to my homework," Jessa said finally.

"Yeah. I guess you'd better spend your whole vacation on it or you're never going to get finished," Cheryl agreed. "Getting started early is probably the smartest thing you'll do over Christmas."

"At least I'm doing my homework on my own. I don't cheat and get my university brother to do it for me!"

"Yeah, right. Just because the only book your family reads is the phone book isn't my problem."

"Just shut up!"

"Fine. Goodbye." There was a click at the other end of the line. Jessa couldn't believe what had just happened. She and Cheryl sometimes squabbled but nobody ever hung up on anybody.

Jessa slammed the phone down. Some friend.

She wrote in big, black, angry letters:

CHERYL IS A TOTAL JERK!!!

This was definitely shaping up to be the worst Christmas ever!

10

Jessa gazed out the bedroom window into the backyard. She could hardly believe her eyes. The snow had continued to fall all night. It lay in soft, pillowy drifts, so deep the seat of the old swing was nearly covered. The whole world seemed to have been repainted in shades of grey and white.

Downstairs, her mother was pouring herself a cup of coffee. Jessa ran into the kitchen, opened the fridge door, and took out the milk.

"Shhh. Your dad's still sleeping."

Jessa didn't quite slam the fridge door, but she didn't exactly close it silently, either.

"He's always sleeping."

Jessa's mother ignored her daughter's snide remark.

"Look what I dug out last night, Jessa." She pointed towards the back door where two pairs of long, narrow skis leaned against the wall.

"Skis!" Jessa said. "Can I go out and try them?"

"Sure. Have your breakfast first. You'll have to use my cross-country ski boots."

Jessa rushed through her breakfast and then put on the

two extra pairs of thick woollen socks her mother offered.

She was sitting on the kitchen floor lacing up the boots when her father walked in. His hair was sticking straight up and his T-shirt was all rumpled.

"Coffee dear?" he mumbled.

Jessa's eyebrows lifted slightly.

"In the coffee pot," her mother answered coolly.

Good, Jessa thought. It didn't look as if they had bonded or anything.

"I'm going skiing," announced Jessa.

"Good idea!" he said. "Snow never lasts more than a day or two around here."

Jessa grabbed the slightly shorter set of skis and poles and clattered out the back door.

She dropped the skis into the knee-deep snow and watched them sink a little. Big white flakes settled like soft kisses on her lips and cheeks as she tipped her head back and stuck out her tongue.

Before long her glasses were wet and splotchy. She pulled a corner of her shirt out from under her thick sweater and tried to dry them but they just got smeary.

Jessa gave up, put her glasses back on, and leaned over to figure out how to fasten her skis onto her boots. By the time she managed to snap the flat toe edge of the low boots into the binding, her fingers were pink from the cold.

The wind blew steadily and the wet snow clung to the north side of the apple tree's trunk. Each black branch had a layer of snow all the way out to its delicate tip.

Standing out in the cold, her feet clipped onto a pair of skis, her hands jammed into the pockets of her jeans for warmth, Jessa could hardly imagine that in only a couple of months the tips of the apple tree branches would be swelling into buds.

The kitchen door opened behind her and her father

came outside carrying the second pair of skis. She wished she hadn't taken so long to get ready.

"What a good way to spend your Christmas holidays!" he said, stepping into his skis quickly and snapping the bindings shut with an expert flick of the tip of his ski pole.

"Come on! I'll race you to the end of the block!"

Jessa picked her poles up out of the snow and stepped forward. The tips of her skis crossed and she fell over sideways into the soft, wet snow.

"Like mother, like daughter," he grinned. "Here, grab this." He held the end of his ski pole out for her to hold on to, but she ignored his offer of help and struggled back up onto her feet by herself.

"You have to glide forward, like this," he demonstrated, sliding one leg forward and bending his knees. "You use the poles for balance and to give you a bit of an extra push."

His skis left two straight tracks in the snow across the backyard. He ducked under the apple tree and skied towards the back fence. Leaning forward he cleared the snow away from the gate and slipped out into the alley behind the house.

Jessa lined her skis up in her father's tracks and followed him slowly. She slid her feet back and forth a little and leaned heavily on her ski poles.

"That's it, honey! Keep coming!"

Jessa cringed. Who did he think he was, calling her "honey"?

Jessa slithered unsteadily through the gate. She had skied past only two or three houses when her father turned the corner at the end of the block. Her attempt to ski faster led to quick disaster as she crashed over into the snow again.

Eventually she reached the end of the alley and looked

along the quiet neighbourhood street, but by then her father had completely disappeared.

Good. She didn't want to go skiing with him anyway.

The street was eerily quiet, muffled as if Jessa were listening with cotton in her ears. A couple of people were out shovelling the snow from their sidewalks and driveways.

As she stood at the end of the alley trying to decide what to do next, one of the neighbours drove slowly along the street in his new truck. At first, the big tires crunched through the snow. Then, as the vehicle approached the stop sign at the corner, it slipped sideways. The driver's face froze in concern until the truck stopped. He relaxed then and looked around to see if anyone had noticed. Jessa smiled and waved.

It was a good thing they had done all their shopping for groceries and presents early this year. Jessa didn't think they'd be driving too far in her mother's little old car until the snow melted.

"Left, right. Left, right," Jessa muttered to herself as she swung her arms and legs and headed for home.

The tracks they had made such a short time earlier were already partly filled with snow. She could see how people could get lost in blizzards.

A few minutes later she wrapped her chilled hands around a steaming cup of hot chocolate her mother had made for her.

"Where's your father?" she asked.

"He took off without me."

"Oh. Well, I guess he'll be back when he gets hungry. Mrs. Bailey called while you were out. She asked if I could bring you down to the barn. She said the chores are taking longer because of the snow."

"I don't think you should drive until it stops snowing,"

Jessa said, remembering the truck sliding on the icy road.

"I know. It doesn't sound as if it's going to stop today. The radio station said another front was moving in and they're expecting more snow."

"I guess we're having a white Christmas for sure!"

"Looks that way, though I'm not quite as excited by that idea as you are. How did the skiing go? Do you think you could get all the way to the barn?"

Jessa shook her head. She thought of how many times she had fallen just trying to get to the end of the alley and back.

"My toes are cold," Jessa said, "even with all these socks."

She peeled the socks off. Her toes were pink and tingling. She rubbed her feet to warm them up.

"No wonder!" her mother said. "Your socks are soaking wet! I'll throw them in the dryer for you."

"I guess I can't ride my bike in this weather, either," Jessa said.

"Not likely. Look, I found these while you were outside."

Her mother held out a pair of mittens and a blue woollen hat. It had ear flaps and a huge white pompom on top. Jessa wondered if any of her school friends were likely to see her wearing it.

"If you and your father help shovel snow this morning, you can spend the afternoon at the barn. I suppose if worst comes to the worst, you can always walk."

"You've got a deal!" agreed Jessa.

11

Jessa trudged down the front steps and out to the sidewalk. The snow was coming down even harder now, and it seemed to be getting darker instead of brighter as the day wore on. Jessa loved their little house on the outskirts of town. Her neighbourhood street with its large lots, older houses, and a fruit tree in nearly every garden was more like living in the country than in the city.

Beyond the end of Jessa's street was a farmer's hayfield and the start of the agricultural area of the Saanich Peninsula.

Once her father returned, they shovelled a path to the sidewalk and then helped the neighbour finish clearing the sidewalk in front of her house.

Finally released from her chores at home, Jessa made her way along the edge of the hayfield. She marvelled at how quiet everything seemed under its blanket of fresh snow. The wind had dropped to a whisper and the heavy flakes fell almost straight down around her.

A row of poplar trees stretched along the edge of the field, a windbreak planted by one of the original farmers who had settled the peninsula. The trees towered above her, their highest branches lost against the grey sky and falling snow.

Eventually, her shortcut brought her to the Dark Creek Railway Trail. From there, it was a quick walk to the barn.

"Thank you for coming, Jessa!" said Mrs. Bailey as Jessa stamped her feet to shake the snow off her boots. "I have to get the tractor going so I can clear the driveway and get out of here. My car can't handle this snow at all!"

Jessa joined Mrs. Bailey beside the little space heater she had brought into the tack room. Jessa took off her mittens and dried them over the warm, orange glow.

"This place sure looks great, Jessa."

It had taken Cheryl and Jessa half of the Sunday before to organize everything perfectly after the paint had dried.

Mrs. Bailey sighed and stretched her back. "I've got to get out and buy some more feed. Those two seem to eat more than everyone else combined!"

"Have you had any luck finding a buyer?" Jessa asked.

"I called the High-Ho people, but they don't need any more horses just now."

"That was a good idea," Jessa said, hoping she didn't sound too guilty. She still felt awful that she had snooped in on Mrs. Bailey's phone conversation.

Mrs. Bailey shook her head sadly. "I've never thought of selling a horse for dog food before, but if I don't find a new home for those two pretty fast . . ."

Jessa's jaw dropped. Dog food! Surely Mrs. Bailey couldn't be serious?

"Trouble is, they're not special at all," Mrs. Bailey went on. "Two, huge, hungry mature geldings. You know, Harpo's sixteen. Who's going to want them?"

"Somebody will," Jessa said quickly. "You just have to get an ad into *Vancouver Island Horse Lovers Magazine.*"

"Do you know how much those ads cost?" Mrs. Bailey asked. "Don't worry," she added, seeing the look on Jessa's face. "I owe Pete at least that much. I'll put a couple of ads in. That was one of the things I was going to do today until my car got stuck up by the house. I even took some photos of the goofy pair."

"What about a notice at the tack store?" Jessa suggested.

"Maybe you could print something up with a space for a photo on your mom's computer," Mrs. Bailey said.

"Sure. I can do that," Jessa said, eager to help save Harpo and Markus from the pet food factory.

"I shovelled a path from the barn to the manure pile," said Mrs. Bailey. "Take each horse out to the cross-ties in turn while you muck out the stall. And you'd better dump the wheelbarrow after each stall because it's getting pretty hard to wheel it through the snow. "I'm going to try and get that stupid tractor going." Mrs. Bailey struggled to finish her sentence before her cough took over. She couldn't speak for a moment.

"Are you okay?" Jessa asked. She didn't think Mrs. Bailey should be out in a snowstorm fixing her tractor. "You should be in bed with a hot water bottle."

Mrs. Bailey wiped her eyes and blew her nose.

"I'm fine. I just can't shake this stupid cold. Now, go get started or we're never going to get the chores done."

Jessa opened the door of the tack room and stepped out into the sheltered walkway that ran along the front of the box stalls. When the horses heard the familiar squeak of the door, four heads appeared over their stall doors.

"There are a couple of bales of straw up in the hayloft," said Mrs. Bailey. "Break one open and take that pony of yours some extra bedding. I checked on him earlier. It's still not perfect in that shelter of his, but it seems to be keeping him dry and out of the wind."

Jessa's stomach clenched. On her way to the barn she had stopped to visit Rebel in his new paddock. He hadn't seemed too concerned about the snow and had picked his way carefully to the gate to greet her.

Even though she didn't want to see the newcomers turned into puppy food, she didn't like the fact poor Rebel was the only horse at Dark Creek who didn't have a proper barn to shelter in during the cold weather.

Jessa pulled her hat down over her ears, glad for the ugly flaps, and waved her arms up and down to get warm. It was really getting chilly.

"Come on, Brandy. I don't have time for this today." Jessa tried to lead Brandy out of his stall to tie him up. The pinto gelding wasn't crazy about working, and sometimes he drove poor Betty King crazy. Today, even getting him to move out of the cozy comfort of his stall was a struggle.

He gave Jessa a dirty look when she snapped him into the cross-ties.

"Don't worry. You don't have to do anything except stand there."

She rolled the wheelbarrow past him into the stall and picked up a manure fork. Mrs. Bailey poked her head around the corner.

"You can give them all some extra hay. It'll help keep their minds off things. I'll put the radio on for you so you can hear what's going on in the world."

As Jessa worked she listened to the C-FIX announcer reporting on the winter storm.

"Don't expect things to get better before they get worse,"

the announcer said. "Police are advising everyone to stay at home and keep off the roads to give snowplows a chance to get caught up. Let's go now to the C-FIX traffic desk."

Jessa worked quickly, listening to the traffic announcer reporting how many accidents there had been in the last twenty-four hours.

"So, folks! It looks like if you haven't got that last-minute Christmas shopping done, it's not going to happen! My traffic advice for this snowy day: stay home for the holidays!"

When Jessa finished Brandy's stall she brought out Billy Jack. She scratched his favourite spot between his eyes and slipped him a piece of carrot from her pocket. Billy Jack was easily the ugliest horse at Dark Creek. It was impossible to tell what his breeding was. His head was clunky and stuck at the end of a neck long enough for a camel. His ears didn't seem capable of standing up straight. They were way too big and flopped out sideways when he relaxed.

Jessa guessed his official colouring was probably a very light palomino, but in truth, he just looked like a very dirty white horse. Sharon Davies adored her old plug and he, in turn, adored her. In the summertime, Sharon threw her old western saddle on Billy Jack and the two of them ambled off happily down the trail.

Billy Jack crunched contentedly, oblivious to the snow falling a short distance away. Jessa gave him a final pat on the neck and went back to work.

She was cleaning the last stall in the big barn when she heard Mrs. Bailey coughing outside. She put her manure rake down and went to the stall door.

At first, Mrs. Bailey didn't see Jessa. She couldn't seem to stop coughing, and when she reached the end of the walkway, she leaned heavily against the wall. Her soaking-wet hair was plastered against her head. Each time she coughed, her eyes squeezed shut and her face flushed a deeper shade of red.

Jessa's heart thumped as she stared at poor Mrs. Bailey, who seemed ready to collapse. Just as Mrs. Bailey straightened up, Jessa stepped out of the stall.

"Jessa!" she wheezed. "I'd better sit down a minute."

Jessa nodded and led the way into the tack room. She plugged in the kettle as Mrs. Bailey sat unsteadily on the tack trunk.

"Oh, my, it's hot in here," Mrs. Bailey said, unwrapping her scarf from around her neck.

Jessa looked at Mrs. Bailey in surprise. The tack room certainly wasn't as cold as being out in the snow, but it was hardly hot.

"Did you fix the tractor?" she asked.

"Hah!" snorted Mrs. Bailey so vigorously she started coughing again. Jessa poured some water into a coffee mug. Mrs. Bailey drank it thirstily, blew her nose, and sighed.

"What a time to be sick!" she said as she dabbed gently at her sore, red nose. "I can't get that stupid tractor to start. The whole thing has seized up and all the tractor places have shut down early for Christmas."

Slumping back against the wall, Mrs. Bailey closed her eyes. Her skin looked dry and hot and she had dark circles under her eyes.

"I sure need my holiday," she whispered.

"Soon. You're leaving soon," Jessa said, wondering if Mrs. Bailey was going to be well enough to go on her trip to Mexico. The tickets had been booked and all the arrangements made for her departure right after Christmas. Jessa could hardly believe Christmas was just around the corner, her father would be leaving, and then Mrs. Bailey would be gone.

Not long after that, her big social studies assignment

would be due. Jessa pushed the thought from her mind. She had enough to think about without worrying about homework.

Christmas Eve was unlike any Jessa could remember. The snow was so deep, even the buses stopped running.

"Why don't we shovel some more snow before I have to leave?" her father asked at breakfast. He and Jessa worked out in the blizzard until their arms and backs ached. Their whole street was completely impassable.

Jessa's mother took it upon herself to see the neighbours were well fed during the storm.

"Coming through!" her mother called out every so often as she pushed past with a platter full of cookies.

Returning from these trips along the narrow path the shovellers had cleared, she stopped and passed on the latest news from the radio.

"The airport's closed until further notice."

"What!?" Jessa and her dad said in unison.

"You mean *nobody* can leave?" Jessa asked.

Her mother shook her head. It was hard to tell what her father was thinking when he heard his flight had been cancelled. Snowflakes fell around them, swirling and dancing before settling lightly on their shoulders.

On her next trip out of the house, Jessa's mom brought chocolate-chip cookies and two mugs of hot chocolate. Gratefully, Jessa stabbed her shovel into the snow and rested for a minute.

"How long do you think it will take you two to clear all the way to the corner?"

Jessa's dad shrugged. "It's slow going. I'd say we'll be busy for most of the day."

"I have a surprise for you two."

"What?" Jessa asked, her eyes sparkling.

"They said on the radio that with all the ice on the power lines there's a good chance some places will lose their electricity."

"So?"

"So, I've decided to cook Christmas dinner today—while everything is still working. This way, your dad can have Christmas dinner with us, even if they open the airport tomorrow."

"Oh," said Jessa glumly. Sharing Christmas dinner with her father didn't seem like such a great surprise. To make things worse, it didn't look as if she was going to be able to get to the barn, either.

The rest of the day passed quickly. All afternoon Jessa and her father helped the other people on the street. Twice they had to climb up on people's roofs to clear away the heavy snow. By the end of the afternoon, all the neighbours were out in the street, trying to shovel it clear in case emergency vehicles needed to get through.

But as long and hard as they worked, when darkness began to fall, there seemed to be nearly as much snow on the ground as when they started, and still the giant flakes fell from the sky, thicker and faster than ever.

"I think we're going to have to call it a day," her father said, turning to make his way back towards the house.

Jessa caught the first whiff of turkey when she was still standing out on the back steps. "I'm starving," she said as she burst in through the kitchen door. "How long will dinner be?"

"Half an hour," her mother said. "You two finished just in time."

Jessa brushed the snow off her jeans. C-FIX was broadcasting the message that the ferries had stopped running and that the airport was likely to stay closed at least until Boxing Day.

Snow had worked its way inside her boots. Jessa peeled off her socks, mittens, and coat, leaving a large puddle of water on the kitchen floor. She listened to the announcer's voice sending a plea for help out into the blizzard.

"We are asking that anyone who is mobile—skiers, snowmobilers, people with chains on their vehicles—get in touch with our volunteer helpline. We have a lot of residents trapped in their homes who need deliveries of food and medicine."

"You know, I haven't forgotten how to ski," Jessa's father said. "I think I'll call them in the morning and see if they still need help."

Jessa's mother nodded in agreement and then looked at her. "Could you wash your hands and then finish setting the table? I put all the Christmas linen out in the living room."

Jessa made a detour via the Christmas tree on her way up to her room. The gifts were arranged neatly under the tree on the red and green cloth that showed up every year in the holiday photographs.

Jessa had been ready for Christmas for weeks. She had shopped early in October for her mother. She hoped her mom would like the china teapot and little cups she had found for her in Chinatown.

The box containing the tea set had by far the fanciest wrapping job under the tree. Jessa and Cheryl had hand-painted sheets of black construction paper using streaks and swirls of Bernie's metallic silver and gold paints.

It had taken them ages to make enough pieces of paper to tape together and cover the box. The final touch was a cascade of silver and gold ribbon strips and dabs of glitter glue that made the whole package sparkle.

Shopping for her father had been a lot more difficult. Jessa had no idea what he liked, and her mother hadn't really been very helpful. In the end, she had found a book about bonsai gardening.

He and his wife lived in a tiny apartment in Tokyo. They only had a small balcony so Jessa thought he probably wouldn't have room to grow anything bigger than a little dwarfed tree.

Jessa poked at a large, rectangular package with her name on it. It was sort of soft. She was about to lift it up and try to feel it more thoroughly when her mother called from the kitchen, "Jessa, leave those presents alone in there!"

Jessa looked guiltily over at the closed door of the kitchen. How on earth did she know what she was doing?

A few minutes later, she carried the pile of freshly ironed linen into the dining room, carefully avoiding the Christmas tree. She shook out the crisp, white tablecloth with all the fancy embroidery.

Every time she saw that tablecloth she felt a little pang. She missed her Omi, her mother's mother, who lived in Germany. The tablecloth had been made by *her* grandmother, about a hundred years ago.

The stitching was a little faded, but the pattern of sprigs of green pine tied with red ribbons was still beautiful. Each matching table napkin had a small wreath in one corner. Jessa couldn't imagine patiently stitching all those little pine needles. Each pine needle had dozens of tiny, precise stitches, each sprig had many, many needles, and there were more sprigs on the whole tablecloth than Jessa had patience to count.

She imagined that her great-great-grandmother must have worked by candlelight. She wondered if her husband and children had appreciated all her hours of labour.

Probably not, she decided. Her great-great-grandmother's family likely believed stitching away late at night was just part of a woman's duties, along with washing clothes by hand and baking bread.

"The Little Drummer Boy" finished with a final *pa-rum-pum-pum-pum* on the radio.

"Batten down the hatches!" the announcer said. "Another front is moving in. Overnight, expect another eight to ten centimetres of snow!"

Jessa laid out the cutlery and placed two candles in the middle of the table. She hummed Christmas carols as she worked.

"It's a good thing most businesses are closed now for the holidays," the announcer said. "Police are advising motorists to stay off the roads, except in dire emergencies.

"We just had a call from an older listener who wants to visit her grandchildren tomorrow for Christmas dinner. Unfortunately, she can't get her car out of her driveway. If there are any listeners out there who would like to help her out tomorrow, give us a call here at C-FIX. If we see a problem, we do what we can to fix it."

Jessa folded the napkins carefully and went into the kitchen to carry out the salad bowl.

"Wow! What a response," the radio announcer said. "Mrs. Willoughby of Oak Bay called just a few minutes ago asking for help getting her car out tomorrow. We've already had six offers of assistance first thing tomorrow morning! Let's just hope it stops snowing and the snowplows clear the roads so Mrs. Willoughby is actually able to drive somewhere! Thanks to all of you who called C-FIX to offer your help."

Jessa's mother clicked off the radio.

"Oh, the table looks lovely, Jessa. Your dad just lifted the turkey out of the oven. Dinner's almost ready."

12

Jessa helped herself to a second portion of turkey and mashed potatoes. She spooned a healthy dollop of cranberry sauce onto the meat.

"Do you have to go to the barn tomorrow?" her father asked.

Jessa had just taken a mouthful of mashed potatoes and gravy so she couldn't answer right away. She shook her head and swallowed.

"No. Marjorie is supposed to come over tonight to get settled in before Mrs. Bailey leaves for Mexico."

Jessa was about to explain that she was going to help Marjorie and Mrs. Bailey on Boxing Day when the lights went out.

"The power!" her mother said.

"You finished cooking dinner in the nick of time," her father said.

The three of them sat silently in the yellow glow of the candles. After a moment of total quiet, Jessa took another bite of her turkey. It was as if her action snapped her parents out of a spell and they started eating again, too.

"Do we have more candles?" Jessa asked.

Her mother nodded. "In the earthquake kit."

Their emergency kit took up two whole shelves of the linen closet.

"Earthquake kit?" her father asked.

"Well, you never know," her mom said, a little defensively. Jessa often teased her mother about the carefully stacked tins, the bottled water, and the big first-aid kit.

Her mother had a neat list of everything she had on hand taped to the door of the closet. She even kept track of the dates she bought supplies. Once a year she bought new tins and replaced all the old ones.

Jessa's mother was studying to be an accountant. It was the perfect career for someone who liked being well organized.

Jessa felt so tired she could hardly sit upright as she finished eating. The soft light of the candles lulled all of them into a companionable silence.

"Well, that was a delicious meal," her father said finally, tipping his chair onto its two back legs. Jessa waited for her mother to tell him he would break the chair sitting like that, but she said nothing.

Instead, her mother picked up one of the candles from the table and held it in front of her as she went down the hallway to fish out what they might need for the evening. She returned a few minutes later with several candles, a package of batteries, and a deck of cards.

"Let's put these in the radio," she said, holding up the batteries. "We can play canasta and listen to the news— after the table gets cleared, of course."

Jessa and her father reached for the bowl of leftover mashed potatoes at the same time, just as Jessa scooped a little bit out of the bowl with her forefinger and popped it in her mouth. Jessa looked guiltily at her mother, who was trying to get the back of the radio open. She hadn't noticed her daughter's fine example of poor table manners.

Her father winked and silently helped himself to a spoonful of cranberry sauce. He carried both bowls out to the kitchen. Jessa led the way, carrying a candle.

Shadows stretched and swayed on the walls as they stacked the dirty dishes on the kitchen counter.

While they made several trips, Jessa's mother lit another half-dozen candles and stood them around the dining room.

Bathed in the warm, golden light, Jessa thought her mother looked quite beautiful. She hoped her father wouldn't notice.

"I'm sure the lights will be back on soon," her mother said, closing the back of the radio and switching it on.

"Well, we're seeing and hearing about lots of problems this Christmas Eve," the announcer said. "Unfortunately, I don't think there's much anyone can do until it stops snowing. Let's go now to the weather forecast."

The forecaster sounded excited and a little out of breath. Jessa wasn't surprised. It wasn't often Victoria got weather like this. In the winter, it rained. In the summer, it was sunny and warm. Boring. Blizzards? Only in Winnipeg.

"Let it snow!" Cindi the C-FIX weather-watcher was saying. "You may as well quit shovelling tonight because Santa's bringing a whole lot more snow later on!"

Jessa's father dealt the cards. Outside, the wind was rising. Every now and then, the windows rattled and Jessa could hear a mixture of snow and icy rain spattering on the glass.

Much later, when she was already in bed, Jessa heard her dad speaking loudly on the phone. The Japanese words clattered out of his mouth as he talked to his wife. As Jessa drifted off she thought it must be a horrible feeling to be trapped away from home at Christmas.

When Jessa woke up the next morning, she thought at first her curtains were closed, the light in her room was so subdued. It was also freezing cold.

She huddled under her covers and shivered.

Usually, Jessa jumped out of bed on Christmas morning, but today, she just curled into a smaller, tighter ball and pulled the blanket up over her head.

When she heard voices from downstairs, she poked her head out from under the covers and looked at her clock radio to see the time.

The face of the clock was dark. Still no power?

Jessa pulled a thick sweater and a pair of jeans on over her pajamas and went downstairs.

"Shhhh," her parents said as she walked into the kitchen. They were both standing stock-still listening to the battery-powered radio.

"I repeat, no public transit buses are running at all today and the Victoria International Airport remains closed. All the Quick-Pick Food Marts are closed, the Victoria Cab Company is not operating today, snowplows are still trying to clear main arteries. . . ."

Jessa opened the back door and gasped. A wall of snow as high as her waist stared back at her and a blast of snowflakes swirled across the kitchen floor.

"Shut the door!" her parents shouted together.

Jessa slammed the door closed. She couldn't believe what was out in her backyard. She had never seen so much snow. Neither, it seemed, had anyone in Victoria.

"The community of Kenwood on the Saanich Peninsula is still without power as are large areas of the

Western Communities. Nothing is moving downtown and we are hearing reports of damage to some roofs due to heavy snow loads."

"Is that the same guy who was on last night?" Jessa asked.

Her mother nodded. "That's Raymond Beardsley. His replacement couldn't get to the radio station last night. He's been up all night. People keep calling in for help. Other people call in to volunteer. This is amazing!"

Jessa's phone rang as Raymond Beardsley continued to list closed businesses, accidents, and travel warnings across Vancouver Island and most of southern British Columbia. She could only imagine how long the list would have been if it hadn't been Christmas Day, when most things were closed anyway.

Jessa said a distracted "Hello" into the phone, then "Hi!" when she realized it was Mrs. Bailey calling.

"Oh, Jessa," she said. "I can hardly see the barn, it's snowing so hard." Mrs. Bailey coughed and coughed. "Marjorie couldn't get here last night. Is there any way you could try to come down and help me?" She coughed again.

Mrs. Bailey sounded really sick and very worried. Jessa thought of the wall of snow waiting outside the back door. It would take hours and hours to get down to Dark Creek, if she could get there at all.

"I could try to ski down," she said doubtfully. With her skiing abilities she'd probably fall into a drift and never be seen again.

"Have a big breakfast and talk it over with your mom. I'll call you back in an hour or so."

13

Jessa joined her parents in the living room. Her father was balancing a piece of bread on a barbecue fork. He poked the whole precarious set-up over the fire. Jessa crouched down beside him in front of the fireplace and leaned closer to the flame. She was still freezing.

"Mrs. Bailey needs me at the barn," said Jessa.

Her parents exchanged worried glances.

"Jessa, I don't think—"

"But I have to go, Mom," Jessa interrupted. "Mrs. Bailey's really sick and nobody else can get there to help her."

"Jessa, I don't think you can get there to help her, either."

"What about the skis?" Jessa suggested. "Or I could just walk."

"Jessa! You can't walk anywhere in all that snow! Don't be ridiculous! Look out there! It's still coming down."

"Who is going to feed the horses?" demanded Jessa.

"Mrs. Bailey is a very capable woman. She'll manage. Maybe her neighbours can help."

Jessa scowled and shook her head stubbornly. Mrs.

Bailey's neighbours were even older than she was.

Jessa took the piece of toast her father offered her. It was nearly black on one side and raw on the other. She slathered peanut butter and jam on the pale side and chewed it with grim determination.

Somehow, she had to figure out a way to help Mrs. Bailey.

"What about calling C-FIX to see if there's someone around here who has a snowmobile?"

"No." Her mother flatly refused to let Jessa near the phone. "Even doctors and nurses can't get to work at the hospitals. We just heard a report of an ambulance getting stuck for four hours! Nobody will blame you if you can't get to the barn to help."

". . . the Victoria International Airport remains closed until further notice. All flights have been cancelled for Christmas Day."

Jessa looked at her parents with shock.

"The airport is *still* closed? When will people be able to leave?" she asked, looking straight at her father.

"Jessa! Don't be so rude!" her mother snapped.

"Susan, it's okay. Maybe I could find a hotel room somewhere."

"Nonsense! You're starting to sound as ridiculous as Jessa! How would you even get to a hotel from here? Both of you, stop this. I know it's frustrating for all of us, but nobody planned a blizzard, did they?"

Jessa and her father exchanged guilty looks.

Jessa's mother tried to reason with her again. "The volunteer coordinators have their hands full with real emergencies. You will not bother them with a silly request like this."

Silly? Jessa couldn't believe what she was hearing.

"Horses can't last long without food. Mrs. Bailey

wouldn't ask for my help if she didn't really need it."

Her mother and father stood side by side, their faces set against her. Without saying another word, Jessa ran up to her room.

I HATE THIS BLIZZARD. Why did I ever wish for a white Christmas? Mom and Dad are being really mean. They won't let me go to the barn.

Jessa lay back on her bed and traced the outline of one of her horseshoes with her finger. Sixteen horseshoes were nailed to the headboard of her bed. Usually, they brought her very good luck.

Her parents just didn't understand how important it was for her to get to Dark Creek. She rolled over on her stomach and wrote some more in her diary.

Cheryl would know what to do. I can't phone her because she's not my friend any more.

Tears welled up in Jessa's eyes as she wrote. She flopped on her back and stared at the ceiling, forcing herself to study the horse poster above her. After what seemed like a very long time, she crawled under her blankets to keep warm. That's where she was going to stay until her parents realized how stubborn and unreasonable they were being.

"Woooo-hooooo!" A thin, cold voice called from outside.

Jessa sat bolt upright in bed and listened.

"Helloooo?" the voice called again.

She ran to her window and looked outside.

"Mrs. Bailey!" Jessa squeaked in shock. "And Harpo!" Jessa raced downstairs, threw open the back door, and peeked over the snowdrift that had swept up against the house.

"What's going on?" her mother asked.

"Mrs. Bailey! What are you doing?" Jessa called.

Harpo stood in snow well over his knees. Mrs. Bailey looked very small sitting astride the great, golden horse. She was riding bareback. Judging by the blinders, Jessa guessed she was using the bridle from Harpo's harness. Mrs. Bailey had snapped a lead shank to each side of the bit.

"I'm here to give you a ride to work, young lady."

Without waiting to check whether it was okay, Jessa turned and ran back inside the house. Quickly, she pulled on a thick sweater, a jacket, and her mother's woolly hat with the pompom. She threw a change of clothes into her small backpack so she would have something dry to wear later.

Jessa pushed past her mother. Mrs. Bailey had managed to manoeuvre Harpo up to the back door. She had clearly presented some pretty compelling arguments about Jessa leaving because Jessa's mother didn't try to stop her.

"Mrs. Bailey offered to let you stay at her house tonight if the weather gets too bad," Jessa's mother said.

Jessa wasted no time. Her mother looked as if she might change her mind at any moment. Jessa reached up and grabbed on to Mrs. Bailey's gloved hand.

"Put your foot on top of my boot and then climb aboard," Mrs. Bailey said.

Jessa half crawled and was half pulled up onto Harpo's broad back. "Ow!" she said as her legs stretched wide to accommodate the huge horse.

"Wait a minute!" her mother said suddenly. "Toothbrush!" She disappeared into the house and returned a minute later with Jessa's toothbrush and a chocolate bar, both of which Jessa stuffed into her coat pockets.

As Mrs. Bailey turned Harpo around and clucked to

him, Jessa's father skied into the backyard with a good-sized backpack on his back. He waved cheerfully.

"I'm off to the emergency coordination centre," he said. "I may as well make myself useful."

Mrs. Bailey and Jessa waved back at him and then continued on their way.

Harpo trudged steadily through the trench he had already made through the snow.

"It should be easier going back," said Mrs. Bailey as Harpo stopped at the edge of the poplars. He dropped his head low and began to feel his way over the uneven ground. In places, the snow drifted as deeply as his belly. It was impossible to see what sort of footing lay ahead.

Several times Jessa clutched Mrs. Bailey's waist, afraid they would all fall and be crushed beneath Harpo's great weight.

"Don't worry, Jessa. You've seen the size of those feet of his. He'll keep us safe."

Sure enough, Harpo seemed to be able to sense what was under his big, hairy feet. Steadily, surely, he plowed his way through the deep snow along the edge of the field. His slow, rolling gait felt most peculiar.

Wrapping her arms around Mrs. Bailey's waist, Jessa snuggled closer. Every now and then she could feel Mrs. Bailey tense up and emit a deep, racking cough. Mrs. Bailey did not seem to be getting any better.

"So? What did Santa bring you?" Mrs. Bailey asked as Harpo turned on to the Dark Creek Railway Trail, where the going was a little easier.

Jessa was stunned. In all the excitement of trying to convince her parents she needed to get to the barn, she had actually forgotten to open her presents!

"I can't believe it!" she said. "I forgot to open them!"

"You what!?" Mrs. Bailey laughed. "How on earth

could you forget to open presents?"

"Well, we were going to do it like we always do, after a Christmas breakfast, except Dad burned the toast and you phoned and then they said I couldn't go to the barn so I went to my room to . . . to . . ." Jessa didn't want to admit she had gone to her room to pout. ". . . so I went to my room to warm up under my blankets. I was lying under my covers and I was just thinking I should go down to finally open the presents when you showed up and then I thought if I didn't hurry up I wouldn't be able to come with you."

The words tumbled out as Jessa related the tale of her strange Christmas morning. She took a deep breath and sighed. It wasn't *exactly* the way it had happened, but it was close enough.

Mrs. Bailey chuckled. "Oh. I see. It was all *my* fault!"

Jessa laughed. "Yeah, I guess so. Kind of . . ."

"It is ironic," agreed Mrs. Bailey, "that with all this snow, it just doesn't feel like Christmas at all." Mrs. Bailey coughed again. Harpo stumbled in the snow and Jessa grabbed at Mrs. Bailey's coat more tightly. The big Belgian quickly recovered his balance and continued plodding on.

Mrs. Bailey let Harpo's lead shank reins go slack. "You see, he knows where he's going," she said. "Just give a horse his head and he'll take you home."

Jessa rested her cheek against the back of Mrs. Bailey's long Australian riding coat. The snowy world moved slowly past them as they made their way along the trail.

Jessa felt Harpo's powerful back and haunches work with each lurching step he took. In places, the soles of her boots just skimmed the surface of the unbroken snow that lay along either side of the track Harpo was plowing with his strong, broad chest.

Jessa was very glad she was not walking all the way to Dark Creek Stables.

14

The snow spun in tiny whirlpools as Jessa lowered herself to the ground at the barn. "Owww," she groaned. Even doing a couple of deep knee bends didn't stretch her legs back into shape. Drifts of powdery snow had blown into the walkway and up against the stall doors in the main barn. She could see where Mrs. Bailey had shovelled a narrow path so she could walk along the front of the stalls to feed and water the horses.

"Hi, gang!" Jessa called out.

Mrs. Bailey rode Harpo across the yard to the little barn. Markus whinnied a loud greeting and Harpo answered with equal enthusiasm.

Jessa could hear Mrs. Bailey muttering to the horses as she slipped Harpo's bridle off and put him back in his stall.

Even though Harpo had plowed his way back and forth through the deep snow several times to make a channel, it still took Mrs. Bailey a long time to join Jessa in the tack room.

Together, they sheltered out of the cold wind.

"As you can see, there's no way we can get the wheelbarrow in and out of the stalls with all the snowdrifts. It took ages to even *find* the wheelbarrow under all that snow!"

Jessa nodded. "What are we going to do?"

"First we have to shovel a better path along the front of the stalls so we can get in there and water. I didn't want to throw hay down the chutes until I had topped up everyone's water."

"Do we have to bring water from the house?" Jessa asked in horror.

Mrs. Bailey shook her head. "The outside faucets are all frozen," she said. "But this one's still okay." She gestured towards the sink in the tack room. "I've left the water running a little. That should stop it from freezing. Unfortunately, all the hoses are frozen solid, so we'll have to carry buckets of water from here out to the stalls."

Jessa grimaced. The thought of hauling buckets of water by hand wasn't too appealing. "I wish the power would come back on," she said.

Mrs. Bailey nodded in agreement. "The worst part is not being able to hear C-FIX. I asked your mother to call us if anything happens we should know about. Now, let's get to work."

Mrs. Bailey opened the tack room door and a blast of icy air swept in towards them. Jessa and Mrs. Bailey looked at each other and then at the piles of snow they had to shovel away. There didn't seem to be anything to say. They each took a shovel and began to dig.

They cleared a path wide enough for the wheelbarrow along the front of the stalls. Even with her mittens, Jessa's hands were freezing and her arms ached from lifting and tossing the snow onto the growing pile that ran the length of the barn.

Poor Mrs. Bailey's face was flushed and red from the exertion. After every few shovelfuls of snow, she had to stop and rest. Her cough sounded awful. Jessa longed to sit down and rest herself, but instead she shovelled harder, hoping they would get done more quickly so Mrs. Bailey could stop and look after her cold.

When they walked back along their newly dug pathway, they were horrified to see that enough blowing snow had already drifted in so that the path was again ankle deep at the point where they had started shovelling.

Mrs. Bailey stayed in the shelter of the tack room and ran water into buckets while Jessa sloshed along the path and then let herself into each of the horse's stalls in turn. She was just steeling herself to make the trip to Babe's stall when the radio suddenly came on.

"Power!" exclaimed Mrs. Bailey.

She immediately stopped running the water and turned on the little heater full blast. Then she plugged in the kettle.

"Warm up in here for a few minutes," said Mrs. Bailey.

Jessa peeled off her wet mittens and rubbed her hands together in front of the small heater.

"Again, we have an urgent request for anyone with a snowmobile in the East Middleton area who can give an ambulance attendant a ride to the fire hall so he can get to work. Please call the volunteer help line if you live in East Middleton and you are mobile. That number again is 555-CFIX."

Just as Jessa and Mrs. Bailey were about to gulp down a quick cup of hot chocolate, the phone rang.

Jessa's mother called to let them know the power was back on all over Kenwood and to see whether they had arrived at the barn safely.

"Jessa?" she said when her daughter took the phone. "Are you okay?"

Her mother sounded worried.

"Sure. Everything's fine."

"You know, you left without opening your presents."

Jessa grinned at Mrs. Bailey. "I know. I can't believe I did that!"

"Well, hard though it is, I will be patient and wait until you get home before I open mine."

"Thanks, Mom."

Jessa had scarcely finished her hot chocolate when Mrs. Bailey started filling the bucket again.

"Off you go," she said. "Give this to Babe and then you'll have to make the big trip to the little barn."

Jessa journeyed back and forth until all the horses in both barns had fresh water.

"What about Rebel?" she asked, holding out the empty bucket to Mrs. Bailey.

"He's okay. There's a ditch at the far end of his paddock. When I rode out to get you, he was pawing through the ice and snow to drink. Take him lots of hay."

Jessa didn't move. "Let me take some water for inside his shelter," she said. "I don't mind making the extra trip."

Mrs. Bailey didn't argue. She filled the bucket and handed it to Jessa.

Jessa struggled through the narrow channel cut earlier by Harpo. It led along the driveway to Rebel's paddock. She crawled over the submerged fence, half swimming and half climbing through the snow. By putting the bucket down in front of her while she moved forward, she managed to get all the way to Rebel's shelter without spilling too much.

"Oh, Rebel, look at you."

Rebel stood quietly inside his shelter, warily eyeing his manger. "What's the matter, boy?"

Jessa peeked inside. Two small brown birds huddled side by side in the shallow wooden tray where Rebel was fed his grain. She smiled and slowly backed away.

"It's okay, Rebel. They won't hurt you—they're just waiting out the storm like you."

She rubbed his neck and gave her horse a little kiss on the muzzle. But Rebel was not so easily comforted. Even when she returned with an armload of tasty hay, he refused to come out of his shelter to greet her. She put the hay on the ground as far away from the manger as possible and he took a grateful nibble.

"Oh, Rebel, this storm will be over soon," she said.

He grabbed the handful of hay she held out to him and munched half-heartedly. It was surprisingly warm inside his small shelter. The wind was blowing from the north and the opening was to the south, so the worst of the drifting had happened on the back side of the shelter.

Jessa checked Rebel's old New Zealand rug to make sure it was still snug, gave him a final rub on the neck, and then left him eating his hay.

It was much easier to give hay to the horses in the main barn. Jessa simply climbed the ladder into the loft and dropped a couple of flakes of hay down through the small trap doors directly above each manger.

"I gave them each a bit of grain this morning before I came for you," said Mrs. Bailey. "They're sure going through a lot of feed in this weather!"

Mrs. Bailey had dragged several bales of hay over to the small barn when it had first started snowing, so feeding Harpo and Markus wasn't too difficult, either.

Cleaning the stalls was another matter entirely. Both barns were totally snowed in. There wasn't really anywhere to put the horses while their stalls were mucked out.

Mrs. Bailey and Jessa worked quickly and quietly around the restless animals. They picked up what they could and then tipped the full wheelbarrow at the very end of the barn.

"We can't get to the manure pile!" said Mrs. Bailey.

"When the storm lets up, we'll have to move all this with the tractor."

The next problem that presented itself was replenishing the shavings. Usually, each horse got nearly a wheelbarrow full of fresh shavings each day.

Jessa looked doubtfully across the unbroken snow at the shavings shed, an impossible fifty metres away.

"Go and get Harpo," said Mrs. Bailey, holding out a halter to Jessa. "I'm feeling very poorly. I have to go and sit down for a few minutes out of the cold. Let him break a trail for us so we can get back and forth to the shed."

"You want *me* to lead him?"

"No, you silly thing. That would be a good way to get trampled. Hop on his back and just neck rein with the lead shank. He's actually very obedient."

"But—"

"No buts. Just go and do it. He'll be pretty worn out from our ride earlier. He won't give you any trouble."

Jessa did as she was told. She had to stand on the hay manger to pull the halter over his big head.

Just hop on him? Jessa looked at the giant horse in front of her. How on earth was she supposed to do that? He was twice as tall as Rebel and she usually used a mounting block even for her pony.

She looked around the barn and spotted two hay bales stacked just inside the main door. Snow had blown in through the door and partially covered them but Jessa was still able to scramble on top.

She coaxed Harpo forward and when he was in front of her, she grabbed a fistful of mane and leaped aboard. Sprawling across his withers, she struggled to swing her leg over his back. Her fingers twisted into his thick mane, holding tight while she tried to get organized. Throughout the entire performance he stood patiently.

"Oh, boy," she moaned as she stretched her leg over his back. When she was finally ready, he carefully picked his way across the yard. When Jessa lay the lead shank across his neck, he obediently turned towards the shavings shed and plowed into the unbroken snow. Jessa grabbed his mane with both hands and hung on for dear life. Harpo put his head down and muscled his way through.

With each heaving step he rolled from side to side. Jessa felt the rhythmic tensing and rippling of his powerful muscles as they flexed and strained to push through the deep snow. Her legs felt increasingly stretched with each step he took. She was definitely going to be bowlegged before the day was out!

Jessa let him rest a minute when they reached the shelter of the shed. Then she turned him around and they retraced their steps. They repeated the trip twice more. Each time, it became a little easier as Harpo's great, wide feet compacted the snow. Jessa gave Harpo's neck a solid pat and put him back in the barn. The trench was wide enough for Jessa to walk through with a garbage bag half filled with shavings slung over her shoulder. Before long, she had lost count of how many times she had travelled back and forth between the barns and the shavings shed.

She worked alone. The one time she stopped to see how Mrs. Bailey was doing, the older woman was sitting slumped backwards against her big tack box, in front of the little heater. At first, Jessa thought Mrs. Bailey might be dead! But then, she saw Mrs. Bailey's chest rise as she took another laboured breath.

Poor Mrs. Bailey, Jessa thought as she backed out of the tack room, closing the door softly behind her as she went. She hoped everything was going to be back to normal when it was time for Mrs. Bailey's flight to Mexico.

15

On her last visit to the shavings shed, Jessa climbed up onto the old-fashioned cutter. The seat was quite comfortable. It was even a little springy when Jessa bounced up and down.

What a funny thing to leave to someone who lived in Victoria, Jessa thought. She smiled to herself at the irony of actually having so much snow the horses probably wouldn't be able to pull the cutter, even if she and Mrs. Bailey could figure out how all the pieces of harness fit together.

After she had unpacked the rig, Mrs. Bailey had taken everything apart and then cleaned and oiled every last strap and buckle. Then, studying a diagram in a dog-eared old book that had been in the harness trunk, she had carefully put it all back together again and draped the harness over two old sawhorses in the shavings shed.

When a particularly strong gust of wind rattled the whole shed, Jessa decided to go back to the tack room to wake up Mrs. Bailey. Jessa hadn't noticed it before, but suddenly she was very, very hungry. No wonder! It was beginning to get dark already. Jessa's piece of toast from earlier in the day had long ago been used up.

Back in the warmth of the house, Jessa and Mrs. Bailey fixed grilled cheese sandwiches and hot chocolate. They sat side by side on Mrs. Bailey's soft couch in the living room.

"I am so tired," said Mrs. Bailey, stroking Eric's head. The round, fluffy cat purred and closed his amber eyes. In the background, C-FIX Radio was broadcasting the latest news on the storm. All of southern Vancouver Island was totally paralyzed. There was no relief in sight. Even more snow was predicted for the coming night.

"Travellers are warned that the airport is closed, all highways leading to Victoria are impassable, and the B.C. Ferry Corporation has cancelled all sailings to Vancouver Island. Many of the smaller Gulf Islands are still without power."

When they had finished dinner, Jessa helped Mrs. Bailey make a fire in the hearth. Crackling yellow and gold flames danced and licked the logs, warming the little living room.

Jessa phoned her mother to let her know she would stay over at Mrs. Bailey's. She heard that her father's quick skiing was proving to be very useful in the storm. He had delivered bread to elderly residents in a nursing home and several tins of formula to a young woman with a new baby.

"He's already asleep on the couch or I'd let you talk to him."

"That figures," said Jessa. "Well, say Merry Christmas to him from me," she added, feeling just a little proud that she knew someone who had helped out in the storm.

Later that evening, Mrs. Bailey brought Jessa a thick, cozy blanket and a pillow. Jessa snuggled into her warm nest on the couch in front of the fire. Ariel, Mrs. Bailey's other cat, hopped up and curled herself into a warm, purring ball on Jessa's stomach.

Mrs. Bailey left the radio playing quietly, even after she went to bed. Jessa was glad of the company. It was very strange sleeping in Mrs. Bailey's living room.

A couple of times during the night, Jessa woke to hear more reports of medical emergencies, collapsing roofs, and always, the endlessly falling snow, smothering the very life out of the dark, silent city.

Jessa woke the next morning to the sound of Mrs. Bailey coughing in the kitchen. Ariel had disappeared and the fire had gone out. Jessa got up and looked out the window. A few flakes still fell, but the sky looked a little brighter, a little less heavy and threatening.

"Did you hear that request on the radio earlier?" Mrs. Bailey asked as Jessa came into the kitchen.

Jessa shook her head. "I guess I was still sleeping."

"It was from somewhere near the golf course. A diabetic dropped her insulin bottle on her kitchen floor and it broke. She needs some more brought from the Kenwood Elementary School."

"From the school?" Jessa asked, confused.

"The roof of the shopping centre collapsed early this morning. The school principal opened the school and has a team of volunteers set up in the gym to distribute emergency supplies. Shhh, listen."

"And in Kenwood, an army of volunteers shovelled a path to the doors of the school. The few community residents who are able to get around on skis and snowshoes have been bringing loads of food and medicine to the emergency shelter in backpacks and on toboggans."

The radio cut to the voice of Mrs. Dereks, the school

principal. She sounded exhausted and close to tears.

"I've never seen anything like it," she said. "Even the army still can't get here to help. But our neighbours and friends are pulling together to get through this."

Raymond Beardsley came back on the air. "Mike Richardson, a volunteer, arrived on skis at the Kenwood Elementary School a short time ago with a small load of emergency medical supplies on his back. The insulin the volunteers have been waiting for was one of the items in that backpack. If there is anyone out there listening to us who has a snowmobile and could deliver a bottle of insulin to the Kenwood Greens Golf Course area, please give us a call at 555-CFIX."

Jessa looked at Mrs. Bailey. "The golf course isn't far from here."

Mrs. Bailey nodded. She and Jessa looked at each other.

"Do you think . . ." Jessa started to ask.

"The cutter?" Mrs. Bailey asked at the same time.

"Let's go feed and water," said Mrs. Bailey. "Then, we'll see if we can figure out how to hitch those two horses to the cutter."

Jessa quickly ate her toast and gulped down a big glass of milk, the last that Mrs. Bailey had on hand. Jessa wondered how long it would be before the stores opened again so they could get more food.

It wasn't easy rushing to do the chores. Once again, Harpo plowed through the deepest drifts with his broad chest so Jessa and Mrs. Bailey could navigate between the two barns and the shavings shed.

The two worked steadily without a break, all the while listening to C-FIX. Reports of lost animals, collapsing greenhouses, and residents trapped in their homes without enough food poured into the radio station.

Just as fast, calls came in with offers of help. Raymond

Beardsley *still* hadn't been able to leave the radio station. During the night he had caught a few hours' sleep on the newsroom couch, but by dawn he was back at his microphone, cheerfully relaying information back and forth across the airwaves.

"Oh, no!" said Jessa in horror after she had topped up Brandy's water bucket. Mrs. Bailey came to stand beside her and together they looked out over the yard. Broad, flat snowflakes were falling thickly again. Jessa thought she had never seen a scarier sight. When was it going to end?

"It's a good thing Pete had this book in the harness trunk," said Mrs. Bailey, thumbing through the old manual on the care, hitching, and driving of draft horses.

Harpo and Markus stood quietly just inside the shed, munching hay. Jessa examined one of the big, stiff collars that Mrs. Bailey had hung on two hooks on the wall.

"Make sure you put the right one on the right horse," she said.

Jessa took the slightly larger collar down from its hook and went to Harpo's head.

"Should I unbuckle it?" she asked.

Mrs. Bailey looked up from her book. "Try slipping it on over his head," she said. "Turn it around—no, the other way," she directed.

Jessa managed to get the collar facing the right direction. She stood in front of Harpo and looked up. "I don't think I can reach. . . ."

Mrs. Bailey came to her rescue. "Let's stand on these," she said, climbing onto one of the sawhorses. Between the two of them they managed to slip it over Harpo's ears.

"Now, we have to twist it up the right way," Mrs. Bailey directed.

They slid the collar around Harpo's wide neck until the buckle was at the top. Then Jessa pushed it the rest of the way down until it rested snugly against his shoulders.

"Good boy," she said. Harpo seemed totally oblivious to what was going on and just kept eating.

Mrs. Bailey rested the book open on the seat of the cutter. By balancing on two overturned buckets they were able to lift the rest of the heavy leather harness onto Harpo's back.

Slowly and methodically, they worked their way from front to back of Harpo's harness, adjusting, tightening, and pulling until all the pictures in the book pretty well matched the horse standing in front of them.

"Can you imagine doing this every morning before going out to plow your field?" Mrs. Bailey asked.

Jessa shook her head and lifted the other collar down for Markus.

Harnessing the second horse went more quickly. When Mrs. Bailey had pulled Markus's short tail over the breeching and adjusted the crupper, she told Jessa to go back to the tack room and call C-FIX to see if they still needed any help ferrying supplies around Kenwood.

Raymond Beardsley answered the phone. Jessa's stomach felt all queasy when she realized she was on the air.

"Hi, my name is Jessa," she said nervously. "We have a team of draft horses and a sleigh—I mean, a cutter— and we're near Kenwood and we were wondering if we could help."

"Horses?" Raymond Beardsley sounded surprised. "Did you say horses?"

"Yes. They get through the snow better than we can."

"Wow! Great! Do you know where Kenwood Elementary School is?"

"Yes," Jessa said. "I'm a student there."

"Wonderful," boomed Raymond. "If you can make your way to the school, I'm sure they can send you out to deliver food or medicine to people who can't get out at all. Thank you *so* much for calling."

Right after Jessa hung up the phone it rang again. It was her mother.

"Jessa! I heard you on the radio. Are you sure that's safe?"

"We'll be fine, Mom. Don't worry."

Her mother paused as if trying to think of a good reason for Jessa not to go. She couldn't seem to come up with one because she said, "I've been baking non-stop since the power came back on. You have to go right past here to get to the school. Why don't you stop by and pick up bread and muffins to take to the emergency shelter with you? You could also pick up your Christmas present. You might need it."

Jessa gathered whatever towels and old horse blankets she could find in Mrs. Bailey's trunk. She loaded them into the cutter as Mrs. Bailey backed Markus into pulling position. Harpo was already hitched to the front of the cutter.

Harpo tossed his head and played with his bit. Markus pawed eagerly at the snow. Even in the shed, snow had blown inside and everything was dusted with a light sprinkling of white.

Mrs. Bailey hooked the horses together. She gave everything one final check to make sure the traces were secure and the horses were neither too far apart nor too close together, and were the right distance in front of the cutter.

When everything seemed set, Mrs. Bailey climbed up on the cutter seat beside Jessa, picked up the lines, and clucked to the team.

"Come on, boys! Git up!"

Harpo and Markus leaned into their collars and easily pulled the little cutter clear of the shavings shed. Jessa tucked a horse blanket over Mrs. Bailey's knees and felt herself being jerked back as the cutter lurched forward.

The horses slogged forward into the chest-deep snow, their heads bobbing up and down with each short, powerful step they took, setting their harness bells jingling.

As they made their way down the driveway past Rebel's paddock, Jessa could hear a whinny from his little shelter.

"We'll have to clear the snow off there later," said Mrs. Bailey, nodding in Rebel's general direction. The snow on top of the roof was more than a metre deep.

Jessa hid her hands under the blanket to try to warm them up. The horses pulled the cutter slowly but steadily along to the end of the driveway and then out into the middle of Arbutus Road.

"You won't see this too often," remarked Mrs. Bailey.

As far as Jessa could see, the white blanket of snow covered everything. It was so deep, the mailboxes and fence posts had completely disappeared.

The team waded along, soothing Jessa with the rhythmic sounds of harness creaking, bells jingling, and runners swooshing through the deep, powdery snow.

16

Jessa staggered along the path to the school. The box of bread, cookies, rolls, and muffins her mother had baked was heavy. When she was halfway between the team out in the snow-covered road and the front doors of the school, a young man came running to help her with her load.

"You must be Jessa! The girl on C-FIX with the horses."

Jessa nodded and flushed.

"Come on in," he said. "We still haven't found anyone who can drop off that insulin. It's too far to send a skier—do you think the horses could make it?"

Jessa nodded. "I think so. They didn't really have too much trouble getting here."

Jessa followed the man into the school. It seemed strangely quiet without hundreds of kids running through the hallways.

The gym, though, was a hive of activity. Tables were set up all around the gym, each with piles of blankets and clothes, tins of food, water jugs, and flashlights. Mrs. Dereks was up on the stage talking to two women in ski jackets. She spotted Jessa and ran down the steps to talk to her.

"Jessa! I'm so glad you're here! Did you come all by yourself?"

Jessa shook her head and explained that Mrs. Bailey was waiting outside with the horses.

"Do you think you could make it over to Barrymore Lane? Behind the golf course? We have the insulin—we just can't get it to the woman who needs it. The snow is really deep down that way and there aren't any roads cleared out in that direction. All our skiers are still ferrying supplies from the shopping centre. Here's Mrs. Brown's address."

As Mrs. Dereks talked, she moved efficiently around the tables. "Here," she said. "This package has everything Mrs. Brown needs: insulin and some more syringes. She said she had almost run out of those, too."

Jessa turned to go.

"Wait!" called Mrs. Dereks. "Take this, too. In case you have trouble."

Mrs. Dereks handed Jessa a cellular phone. "Just push the green button when it rings or when you need to make a call," she instructed. "Our number here is taped onto the back. Or, if you really get into trouble, call C-FIX."

"I know," said Jessa. "If they see a problem, they try to fix it." She liked the station's slogan. It was so optimistic.

Jessa ran back out to where Mrs. Bailey was waiting with the team.

"Let's go," she said, feeling more as if she were in the middle of an adventure movie than in her own life.

Mrs. Bailey raised the lines a little and let them fall on the horses' rumps. Their muscles tensed and they leaned forward, getting the cutter moving again.

As they made their way along the long, winding road that followed the curve of the golf course, Jessa inspected the brand new New Zealand rug that had been in the big package under the tree. Her mother had handed it to her when Jessa had picked up the baking to take to the school.

"Do you think it will fit Rebel?" Jessa asked Mrs. Bailey.

"I know it will because I told them what size to get."

Jessa read the card. "Merry Christmas. Love, Mom and Dad."

She spread the new winter horse blanket over Mrs. Bailey's knees.

Mrs. Bailey clucked encouragement to the two horses.

"No wonder nobody could get back here," said Mrs. Bailey when they finally turned on to Barrymore Lane. The street was narrow and had only about four houses on it. It seemed that maybe someone had once subdivided an old farm.

The golf course was just visible beyond the end of the cul-de-sac like a scene from a Christmas card.

Jessa peered at the darkened windows of the houses on the street. She couldn't see any signs of life. It was like a scene out of an alien abduction movie. Jessa suspected it was more likely that everyone had gone away for the holidays. The snow in the street was completely unbroken.

There was a white lump at the very end of the road. Jessa suspected it might be a car, but she couldn't tell for sure.

Jessa held the emergency package carefully on her lap and watched out for the house numbers. Sure enough, Mrs. Brown's house was the one with the buried vehicle.

"Whoa, boys," said Mrs. Bailey, pulling the horses to a stop in the middle of Mrs. Brown's front yard. The bungalow was just as dark and eerily quiet as the others on the sleepy street.

"I hope we're not too late," said Jessa nervously.

"You're going to have to make it the rest of the way to the front door," said Mrs. Bailey. "I can't get them any closer." She coughed deeply.

Jessa looked at her with concern. Mrs. Bailey didn't seem any better. In fact, she looked quite a bit worse.

Mrs. Bailey smiled weakly at Jessa. Her face was flushed and Jessa saw her hands were shaking as she tucked the lines in front of her so they didn't slip away into the snow. Mrs. Bailey jammed her gloved hands into the pockets of her long coat.

"Just cold, is all," she said. "Now, hurry up!"

Jessa did as she was told and stepped out of the cutter. Right away she sank up to her armpits in snow. She held the package with the insulin up above her head and, using her other arm for balance, moved slowly towards the house. With each tiny step, she twisted from side to side to help clear the way.

"Hello!" she shouted. "Are you okay?"

After every couple of steps, Jessa stopped to catch her breath. She leaned against the wall of snow beside her and tried to ignore the aching numbness in her toes.

Finally, she reached the front steps and rang the doorbell. Only silence answered from inside the darkened house.

Maybe she had the wrong house number?

Jessa rang the doorbell again. Mrs. Bailey, still huddled in the cutter, made a knocking motion with her hand.

Jessa took off her mitten and knocked as hard as she could on the front door.

Had Mrs. Brown tried to go for help? But no tracks led away from the house. She *had* to be in there.

Jessa's heart lurched. What if the woman had fainted or something? Didn't diabetics faint?

With her heart pounding, Jessa tried the door. The knob turned and the door swung open.

"Hello? Are you in here?" Jessa called into the quiet house.

She listened carefully. She thought she could hear water running somewhere.

"Mrs. Brown?" she called again.

This time she heard a sound from somewhere along the hallway. She froze and the hairs tingled on her arms. Then she heard it again: a long, low groan. It sounded like someone was dying.

17

Without stopping to think, Jessa ran down the hallway. "Mrs. Brown? Where are you?" she called.

She ran into a bedroom. It was empty, but the groaning was louder. Slowly, Jessa walked around the bed towards the open door of an adjoining bathroom.

The woman on the bathroom floor looked awful.

"I can't stop throwing up," she groaned. "Oh, please help me."

Jessa was horrified. She didn't know what to do. Mrs. Brown looked older than her mother, with dark brown, shoulder-length hair. She was slumped against her bathroom cabinets. Her eyes were closed and she hardly seemed to be breathing. She didn't even seem to care that a total stranger was standing in her house.

"I . . . I . . . here's your insulin," Jessa offered, her voice shaking.

The woman on the floor didn't answer.

What if she was too late? Jessa thought in a panic. What should she do?

"Call a doctor," the woman whispered from the floor.

Jessa felt the cellphone in her pocket. Maybe someone at C-FIX would know what to do, whom to call.

"Hello?" Jessa said into the phone, all the while warily watching Mrs. Brown. She thought that maybe, if she didn't take her eyes off the woman, she wouldn't die.

"This is Jessa. I'm here with the insulin but I don't think Mrs. Brown is well enough to take it," she said. It was all she could do not to start crying. She kept staring at Mrs. Brown's crumpled bathrobe and the way her hair hung forward and half hid her face.

"Hold on a second, honey," said the voice at the other end of the line. "We have a paramedic here at the station. Let me put him on."

Mrs. Brown groaned deeply and held her stomach.

Jessa's heart jumped in horror. What if she died right there on the bathroom floor?

"I'm calling for help," Jessa said, trying to sound confident and reassuring. "Hang on . . . just hang on. . . ."

Mrs. Brown's head rolled sideways a bit.

"Hurry up," Jessa whispered into the phone.

A moment later a man's voice came on the line.

"Jessa. You are going to have to do exactly as I tell you. Mrs. Brown needs her insulin now. If she doesn't get it, she could slip into a diabetic coma. Do you understand?"

Coma? Jessa swallowed and closed her eyes. This couldn't be happening!

"But she's throwing up! Maybe she just has the flu."

"Jessa, listen—that happens when a diabetic's blood sugar gets very high, dangerously high. Do you think she can give herself a shot?"

Jessa looked doubtfully at the woman on the bathroom floor. She looked like maybe she was already in a coma. She wasn't moving at all. Jessa tried to swallow again but her mouth was completely dry.

"I don't think so," she said in a small, frightened voice.

"Then you'll have to do it," the paramedic said.

"I can't!" Jessa said, panic rising in her voice.

"Isn't there a grown-up with you?" the man asked.

Jessa thought of poor Mrs. Bailey waiting outside in the snowstorm.

"Mrs. Bailey is out with the horses. Maybe I could go and get her. It'll take a while, though. The snow's pretty deep out here and she's kind of sick, too."

"There's no time, Jessa. You are going to have to do it. You don't have a choice. Every minute counts. Now, listen carefully."

The voice at the other end of the line instructed Jessa on how to clean the top of the new insulin bottle, and then how to carefully poke one of the new syringes in through the rubber top.

His voice was calm and reassuring and he made Jessa repeat back his instructions for each step.

When she had drawn up the correct amount of insulin, he told her to go to Mrs. Brown's side.

"Mrs. Brown?" she said. "Here's your shot. Do you think you can give it to yourself?"

Jessa's hand shook as she held out the syringe. For a long, horrifying moment, Mrs. Brown didn't say anything. How on earth was Jessa going to give her the injection?

But then Elizabeth Brown opened her eyes, took the syringe, and injected the dose into her thigh. The whole process was over so quickly, it was obvious she had done it hundreds of times before.

Jessa didn't say anything. She knelt beside Mrs. Brown on the bathroom floor, the cellular phone tucked between her cheek and shoulder.

"She did it herself," she whispered with relief.

She heard the man on the other end of the line draw a

deep breath. "Good. Excellent, Jessa."

Jessa didn't take her eyes off Mrs. Brown.

"She doesn't look any better," she said.

"It will take about half an hour to start working. Can you see if she'll drink some water while you're waiting? She'll be fine, Jessa. Do you think you can wait with her until she seems better? We have another medical emergency on another line. Call us right back if anything changes."

Jessa found a glass in the kitchen and came back to Mrs. Brown's side. She still hadn't moved from where Jessa had first found her.

Gently, Jessa held the glass to the woman's lips.

"Here," she said softly. "Drink some of this."

Mrs. Brown sipped the water Jessa offered and then groaned deeply. Jessa put the glass on the bathroom counter and went back to the front door. It was still wide open.

18

Mrs. Bailey sat hunched forward in the cutter. She straightened up and waved anxiously when she saw Jessa standing in the doorway.

"Is everything okay?" Mrs. Bailey called.

"I hope so," answered Jessa. "We have to wait for the shot to work," she added, not quite believing what had just happened. "You'd better come in."

Mrs. Bailey thought about it for a moment and then nodded her head. "I'll move as close as I can with the horses."

While Mrs. Bailey manoeuvred the team, Jessa went to the bedroom and sat uneasily on the edge of the bed. Mrs. Brown still hadn't moved out of the bathroom.

What if the insulin didn't work? Jessa wondered. What if something else was wrong?

Jessa wished there was something else she could do. Waiting was the worst thing she could imagine. She heard the front door open as Mrs. Bailey let herself in. Jessa felt better just knowing she was there.

"Would you like some more water?" Jessa asked Mrs. Brown after what seemed like ages.

"Yes, please," Mrs. Brown answered quite clearly. "Thank you, dear," she said, sitting up a little straighter and drinking the water Jessa offered. She rested her head back against the bathroom cabinet.

"Oh, I feel just awful," she said. Then she opened her eyes and looked at Jessa.

"Who *are* you?" she asked suddenly.

Jessa smiled. "Hi. I'm Jessa Richardson. I brought the insulin with my friend Mrs. Bailey and her two horses."

"Thank you for coming," said Mrs. Brown gratefully. "I heard about you on the radio."

Jessa couldn't believe how fast Mrs. Brown seemed to be getting better.

"I dropped my insulin on the kitchen floor last night," she explained. "I thought I'd be able to get out and buy some more this morning but with all this snow . . ."

Mrs. Brown stopped mid-sentence. Then, she started to stand.

"Are you sure you should get up?" Jessa asked.

"Well, I can't stay in the bathroom all day, now, can I?"

Mrs. Brown made her way unsteadily to the kitchen. She leaned heavily against the counter and made herself some cheese and crackers and poured herself a large glass of milk.

"Would you like anything, dear?" she asked Jessa.

Jessa shook her head. She was totally amazed at what was happening. She had arrived with the insulin less than an hour earlier and already Mrs. Brown was moving around her kitchen, making lunch almost normally.

Mrs. Bailey poked her head into the kitchen.

"Hello. I'm Barbara Bailey—excuse me for being so rude, but I have to keep an eye on the horses." She disappeared back into the living room.

"Let me make you two some lunch," said Mrs. Brown.

"Are you sure you're okay?" Jessa asked.

"Of course. It's the least I can do. I'll also make a Thermos of tea you can take with you. After all, you two came all the way out here for me."

Altogether too soon, Jessa and Mrs. Bailey had to leave the warmth of Mrs. Brown's living room and head back out into the snow. They didn't leave empty-handed. Mrs. Brown insisted they take along a big package of chocolate-chip cookies for the road and some carrots for the horses. The tea was piping hot with milk and honey, just the way Mrs. Bailey liked it.

"I'll call the radio station and let them know every-thing's okay," said Jessa as they pulled the horse blanket back over their knees. Beside her, Mrs. Bailey couldn't seem to stop shivering.

"Drink some tea," Jessa said. Mrs. Bailey didn't argue. Jessa put her hands in her pockets to warm them up and felt the chocolate bar her mother had given her.

She pulled it out and broke off a big piece for Mrs. Bailey, who ate it gratefully and took another swig of tea. Jessa thought she looked a tiny bit better.

"Do you think you could drive them back to the school?" Mrs. Bailey asked.

Jessa tucked the new horse blanket closer around her travelling companion and shook her head. "We're not going back to the school. I'll just give them their heads and they'll take us home."

Mrs. Bailey smiled weakly and nodded. Her eyes closed and she rested her head against the back of the seat.

The drive back to Dark Creek took more than an hour. The whole time, Mrs. Bailey didn't say a word. She drifted in and out of an uneasy sleep for most of the journey.

She didn't even say anything when Jessa had to stop the team in a couple of particularly deep places to clear away accumulated snow from in front of the cutter. The first time she spoke, in fact, was when they turned on to the driveway.

"I'll sit in the tack room and warm up for a few minutes, Jessa. Do you think you can put the boys away? Dry them off as best you—" A coughing fit overtook her and Mrs. Bailey couldn't finish her sentence.

"It's okay," Jessa said. "I'll put them away."

"Oh, no! Look at that!" Mrs. Bailey sputtered between coughs.

Jessa looked where Mrs. Bailey was pointing. Nearly two metres of snow had accumulated on top of Rebel's shelter.

"I'll rest a few minutes," wheezed Mrs. Bailey. "Then, we'll have to try to clear that off before his shelter collapses. Stop, Jessa!"

"Whoa, boys."

Jessa heaved on the lines. The horses weren't too happy about stopping so close to the cozy warmth of their stalls.

Mrs. Bailey struggled with Rebel's awkward New Zealand blanket.

"Put this on him." She leaned out of the cutter and put the new blanket on the top rail of the fence, the only rail visible above the snow.

Jessa dropped Mrs. Bailey off at the tack room and then drove the team forward to the shavings shed. Her fingers ached with the cold as she worked the stiff buckles and straps of the heavy harness. Several times she lost her balance and nearly fell off the sawhorses. She was so tired she wanted to sit down and cry.

Getting the heavy collars off by herself was nearly

impossible but she finally managed to drag them off each horse in turn.

Jessa forced herself to keep moving until Harpo and Markus were safely back in their stalls. She towelled them off as well as she could, checked their water buckets, and gave them extra hay.

On her way back across the yard she heard a phone ringing. The cellular phone! Jessa had forgotten all about it. It was Raymond Beardsley checking to see how everything was going.

"Congratulations, Jessa," he said.

"Why?" she asked.

"You're quite a hero!" he said. "Elizabeth Brown called a while ago to make sure we thanked you properly for saving her life."

Jessa didn't know what to say. A thousand pressing problems crowded her mind. She had to get Mrs. Bailey up to the house and clear the snow off Rebel's roof before it collapsed on him.

Rebel's roof! "Mr. Beardsley? Do you think someone could maybe help me to clear off a shed roof?" She looked back over her shoulder at Harpo and Markus's small barn. There was quite a pile of snow on there, too. "Actually, there are two outbuildings that don't look so good." Jessa tried to keep the quiver out of her voice. "I don't know if I can do all that on my own."

"Don't worry, Jessa. I'm sure we can get someone out there to help you. Don't climb up on the roof if you're alone. Okay?"

"Okay," Jessa promised. She gave him the address and then hung up the phone. Suddenly, Jessa felt small and alone standing in the middle of the stable-yard. She made herself get back to work. The other horses had to be fed and their water checked. She worked as fast as she could, horrified that darkness was already beginning to gather. Where had the day gone? When would someone come to help her clear the snow off the roofs?

Twice Mrs. Bailey came out to help water and feed. But both times she was driven back into the tack room by a racking cough that shook her whole body. Jessa worked even harder, hauling water, throwing down hay, carrying out more soiled bedding, bringing in fresh shavings. She put on Rebel's new rug. It fit perfectly.

"There you are," she said. "That should help keep you toasty warm."

She felt horribly guilty when all she had time for was a quick pat on Rebel's neck. The two little birds in the manger had disappeared. Jessa wondered where on earth they would have gone in the swirling snowstorm.

When Jessa finally finished the chores, she went into the tack room. Mrs. Bailey sat wheezing on the tack trunk, her hands held out over the little heater.

"Jessa! Where on earth have you been?" Mrs. Bailey sounded concerned. "Have the horses all been fed?"

Jessa frowned. Of course the horses had all been fed. Mrs. Bailey had been sitting right there when Jessa had climbed up to the hayloft to throw down hay.

"Don't you remember?"

Mrs. Bailey put her hand to her head and closed her eyes. "Of course, dear. For a minute I thought I'd only dreamt that. Are you hungry?"

Jessa nodded. She really didn't like the way Mrs. Bailey was acting. "I think you should go to bed," she said. "Come on. I'll help you up to the house."

Mrs. Bailey didn't protest as Jessa took her arm and helped her to her feet. Jessa clicked off the radio and Mrs. Bailey turned off the dribbling faucet.

"Don't you want to leave that on?" Jessa asked.

Mrs. Bailey looked confused. "Leave the water running? Why?" Then, as if a distant memory was slowly returning, Mrs. Bailey went back to the sink and turned the water back on.

"Yes," she said wearily. "We wouldn't want the pipes to freeze, now, would we?"

Jessa's stomach clenched into a small fist of fear. What was wrong with Mrs. Bailey?

Mrs. Bailey shook her head slowly from side to side. "The horses are fed, right, Jessa?"

"Yes, Mrs. Bailey. Come on. Let's get up to the house."

Usually, the walk from the barn to the house took about thirty seconds. After ten minutes of hard slogging, Jessa began to wonder if she and Mrs. Bailey would ever get there.

If only the volunteers would come, they would help her, Jessa thought. They would know what to do.

The day's accumulation of snow had completely obliterated the trail Mrs. Bailey and Harpo had carefully made up to the house that morning. And still the snow was falling, harder than ever.

19

Darkness crept around them, encouraged to make an early arrival by the heavy clouds and spiralling flakes. Mrs. Bailey stumbled with almost every step. Several times she insisted on sitting down in the snow with her eyes closed.

"Come on, Mrs. Bailey. We have to get to the house," insisted Jessa, tugging on her arm. "Look how cold you are!"

It was true. Mrs. Bailey was shivering violently.

When Jessa reached forward to brush a wisp of wet, grey hair from Mrs. Bailey's cheek, she drew her hand back in horror. Mrs. Bailey's skin wasn't cold at all. It was burning hot! No wonder she wasn't making any sense.

"I think you have a fever, Mrs. Bailey. Come on, right now," Jessa said as firmly as she could. She took both Mrs. Bailey's hands in hers and pulled her to her feet. "Walk! Come on. We're almost there."

Jessa struggled backwards through the snow, dragging and cajoling Mrs. Bailey along.

"Please, Mrs. Bailey. Just a little farther. I'll make you some nice hot tea inside."

When the pair finally staggered through the door, Jessa nearly wept with relief.

"Now, you go right into your bedroom and lie down." Mrs. Bailey obediently went to her bed and lay down without even taking off her coat.

Jessa wondered where she'd find a thermometer. She found one in a drawer in Mrs. Bailey's bathroom and shook it the way she had seen her mother do. Back in the bedroom, Mrs. Bailey had disappeared under a huge pile of blankets.

"Mrs. Bailey, let me take your temperature," Jessa said. A hand reached out from under the covers, took the thermometer and then disappeared again. Every now and then, the mountain of blankets shuddered. About a minute later, the hand passed the thermometer out again.

Jessa went out into the kitchen where the light was better. She turned the thermometer back and forth between her thumb and forefinger until she could see the sharp edge of the silver line right beside the 104 degree mark.

Jessa knew that normal body temperature was 37 degrees centigrade, but she wasn't sure what normal was on Mrs. Bailey's old-fashioned Fahrenheit thermometer. She phoned her mother to find out.

"104 degrees?!" Her mother sounded horrified. "Are you sure?"

Jessa checked the thermometer again. She was sure. Once she had the hang of it, it wasn't that hard to see.

"Jessa, is there another grown-up somewhere around? A neighbour? Anyone?"

Jessa looked out the window. She couldn't even see the lights of the next farm, it was snowing so hard.

"I don't think so," Jessa said. "Some people were supposed to come and shovel snow but now it's pretty dark so I don't think they'll make it here tonight."

"Jessa, you have to find some Tylenol and give a couple to Mrs. Bailey. Make her drink lots of water. I'm going to try to find someone to give me a ride down there so I can help you."

"Okay, Mom," Jessa said in a small, tired voice. "I hate this storm. I wish I had never wished for snow."

"I know, Jessa. It's supposed to stop soon. Make sure Mrs. Bailey stays in bed until I get there. Get a cool, damp face cloth and wipe it over her forehead. We have to try to get that fever down. I'll get there as soon as I can."

An hour later, Jessa heard the back door open.

"Mom?" she called. She could hear the sound of heavy boots.

Jessa came out into the dimly lit hallway and froze in terror. A man in a dark coat stood with his back toward her. She gasped and the figure turned around.

"Dad!" Jessa cried in relief.

"It was faster for me to ski than wait for someone who could bring your mother," he said. "How is she?" he asked, unwinding his scarf and stamping snow off his boots.

"A little better, I think," Jessa said, her heart still hammering. "Not quite so hot. And she stopped talking about the tractor."

"What?" Her father looked perplexed.

"She asked me to move the tractor out of the kitchen," Jessa said. "She's been hallucinating. She thought one of the cats was a skunk."

Her father smiled. "Oh, Jessa. You have been *so* brave."

Throughout the night, Jessa and her father watched over Mrs. Bailey. They brought her water and cool, wet cloths, and when her fever started creeping back up, they gave her more Tylenol. Mrs. Bailey was not exactly helpful. When her temperature crept close to 104 degrees again despite their best efforts, Jessa's dad insisted they take drastic action.

"No, you can't see my legs!" declared Mrs. Bailey indignantly.

Jessa watched the argument with her arms full of dripping towels.

"Mrs. Bailey," her father explained patiently, "we have to wrap wet towels around your legs to bring down your fever."

"Absolutely not! I am freezing cold already."

Jessa raised her eyebrows and looked at her father.

"The fever makes her feel cold. I'll lift the blankets up and you put the towels on her legs."

"I heard that!" said the voice from under the blankets.

"Mrs. Bailey. Let us help you," Jessa pleaded. She thought of how Mrs. Bailey stuck her hand out to take the thermometer rather than let anyone take her temperature for her. "Why don't you just stick your legs out so we can reach them?"

"Oh, fine. If you'll leave me alone after this . . ."

First one and then the other skinny leg emerged from under the covers.

"Ahhh!" cried Mrs. Bailey when the cool, wet towels touched her skin. "That's burning me!"

She tried to kick Jessa's hands away.

"You must lie still!" her father said sternly, placing his hand on the old woman's knee. At the touch of his hand, Mrs. Bailey seemed to relax a bit. "Shhh," he said kindly. "You'll feel much better soon."

The towels worked wonders. When her fever fell a little, Mrs. Bailey drifted into a fitful sleep.

Jessa smiled shyly at her dad. She was glad he had come to help. He seemed to know exactly what to do.

"Jessa! Look at the time. You should sleep for a few hours. You're exhausted."

"Will Mrs. Bailey be okay?"

He nodded. "I'll sit up with her."

Jessa didn't have the strength to argue. She crawled under the blankets on the couch and closed her eyes. Images of the past few days swirled through her mind. The last thing she felt was Ariel hopping onto the couch and curling into a ball beside her.

The next morning, the sun shone for the first time in days. The temperature rose steadily and soon the snow began to melt, filling the air with the sounds of running water.

From the time it first got light, Mrs. Bailey's house was a hive of activity. The first to arrive were the volunteers who came to clear away snow from the roofs.

Jessa's father tended to Mrs. Bailey. He soon had a full-time job on his hands trying to keep Mrs. Bailey in bed. The patient kept trying to get up to help with the chores! Two of the volunteers offered to stay and help with the horses when they realized Jessa was the only one in any shape to work in the barns.

As soon as the volunteers left, a tractor with a snowplow cleared the road and the driveway. Soon after that, a big four-wheel-drive truck arrived to take Mrs. Bailey to the hospital.

"Nonsense!" she protested all the way down the stairs. "I am fine! Just a little cold is all!"

"She's a tough old goat," her father said to Jessa as the truck drove off. "She was coughing up blood last night and that fever just isn't going away. That's why I called someone to come and pick her up. I just know she can't be trusted to stay out of the way and rest."

A little later, Mrs. Bailey called from the hospital. "A touch of pneumonia is all," she said. "Nothing to worry about. They've got me on antibiotics. I'll be out in a day or two."

"I'll stay here and take care of things," Jessa volunteered.

"It's all right, dear. I just called Marjorie. She's coming to take over. I've also called Betty. The fool of a young doctor here says I'm not well enough to travel. There goes Mexico!"

Jessa didn't say anything, but she had to agree with the "fool" doctor.

Marjorie arrived at Dark Creek later in the afternoon. Jessa insisted on staying at Mrs. Bailey's until she had helped Marjorie do the evening feed.

"Come on, Jessa," her father finally said. "You've done more than enough here. It's time to go home."

20

The cleanup after the blizzard started the minute it stopped snowing. As soon as the Pat Bay Highway was cleared, the ferries started running again so travellers could get back and forth to the mainland. The airport opened two days later.

Jessa's father managed to get a new flight booked for late in the day on Thursday. On Wednesday, Suzanna called from the Tack and Feed Emporium.

"Hello? Is this Jessa?"

"Speaking."

"Have you heard the terrible news?" Suzanna asked.

"What news?" Jessa asked.

"One of the High-Ho barns collapsed under the weight of all the snow last night."

"Oh, no!"

Suzanna's voice was grave. "Four horses were so badly hurt they had to be put down."

Jessa's eyes widened with horror.

"I'm calling everyone I can think of to see if they can come and help rebuild the barn. Roslyn is in no shape to organize anything. The Blumens have donated lumber and I already have about a dozen people willing to come out and help."

"Don't call Mrs. Bailey," Jessa said quickly. "She's really sick. She just got out of the hospital but I know she'd want to come and help. I'll bring my dad. We've been helping to shovel out the neighbourhood for the last two days. He'd probably enjoy a change."

Jessa hung up the phone and considered what to do next. She picked up the receiver and dialed Cheryl's number. She wasn't sure if her friend would even want to speak to her again.

"Hi, Cheryl, it's me."

"Jessa! Hi! I heard about you on the radio. You're famous!"

Jessa breathed a sigh of relief and went on, ignoring her friend's gushing. "Listen, Cheryl. I need your help."

She explained what had happened to the carriage horses and the barn and how she and her father needed a ride to the High-Ho barn.

"I'll come and help," Cheryl offered quickly. "I'm sure my dad would give us all a ride. He has chains on his pickup so he's getting around pretty well."

In the back seat of the truck, Cheryl and Jessa exchanged stories about the storm while their fathers compared barn-building ideas.

Jessa suspected neither of the men really knew what he was talking about.

"Jessa?" Cheryl said in a low voice, leaning over close to Jessa's ear.

"What?" whispered Jessa.

"It was all Anthony's fault."

"What was?" Jessa asked.

"The gum."

Jessa had forgotten about the gum incident. "What do you mean?"

"It was *his* gum. I got suspicious because Bernie kept talking about the 'yellow' ick and we were both chewing purple bubble gum. He finally admitted it."

"What!"

"He took it out when he was doing a headstand. He didn't want to choke."

Jessa laughed. "Why didn't he say anything?"

"Because Bernie was so mad. He didn't want to admit it was his fault."

"Oh, no!"

"Bernie got even madder when he confessed. She made him apologize to me on his knees."

"Really!? I wish I could have seen *that!*" Jessa couldn't quite picture Cheryl's brother down on his knees, begging for forgiveness.

"Jessa?" Cheryl whispered.

"What?"

"I'm really sorry I blamed you."

"It's okay," Jessa said. "Let's not be mad any more, okay?"

"And I'm sorry about what I said about your homework."

"You were right, actually. I *still* haven't started."

Both girls laughed and Cheryl gave Jessa a poke in the arm. "You really are hopeless, my dear. Too busy being a heroine, I suppose."

The truck pulled to the side of the road near the High-Ho barns. People were everywhere carrying tool boxes and boards towards the collapsed barn.

The C-FIX van was already there. Rachel Blumen's

father was talking to a reporter. When he spotted Jessa he pointed at her and a man with a microphone came running over.

"Oh, no," she muttered under her breath.

"And here we have another community member who has helped bring us through the worst blizzard of the century."

Jessa listened in embarrassment as he droned on about how she had arrived just in the nick of time with Mrs. Brown's insulin, then driven Harpo and Markus through the blizzard to save Mrs. Bailey's life as well. It all sounded very exaggerated and rather dramatic to her.

It seemed as if the reporter was talking about some other person and not Jessa at all. *She* really hadn't done anything special.

While a reluctant Jessa was being interviewed, Mr. Blumen hovered around in the background. Jessa smiled at him and wondered what he wanted. Mr. Blumen had a reputation for being loud.

When the C-FIX reporter had asked her enough questions, he moved on to interview some of the volunteers who were already working on the barn.

"Hi, kiddo," said Mr. Blumen, seizing her hand and pumping it up and down. "Congratulations! You are one brave young lady."

Jessa's father could see how uncomfortable Jessa was with all the attention she was getting.

"I think Jessa just wants to be left alone," he said.

"Oh? And who are *you*?" Mr. Blumen asked. Mr. Blumen wasn't known for his patience and fine social graces.

"I'm Mike Richardson. Jessa's father."

"I've never seen you around before."

Jessa's father bristled. Mr. Blumen refused to let go of Jessa's hand.

"Come on, Jessa," her dad said.

"Maybe she'd like some hot apple cider," said Mr. Blumen, still gripping her hand tightly.

"Stop it!" Jessa said in a voice that came out much louder than she expected. She blushed and cleared her throat.

"Mr. Blumen, this is my father. His flight was cancelled so he got snowed in. And, Dad, this is Mr. Blumen. He's got a big horse farm not too far from Dark Creek. He worked as one of the volunteer coordinators at C-FIX. He also donated the wood to rebuild the barn," Jessa said, repeating what Suzanna at the tack store had told her.

"He probably hasn't had much sleep recently," she added, hoping that would help explain Mr. Blumen's bad temper. She pulled her hand back and walked away, leaving the two men staring at each other a bit foolishly.

Roslyn of the High-Ho Carriage Co. came up to Jessa as she was shovelling snow away from the side of the barn where two volunteers were trying to erect a ladder.

"Are you the same Jessa who helps Mrs. Bailey over at Dark Creek?" Roslyn asked.

Jessa nodded.

"I'm pleased to meet you. Could you ask Mrs. Bailey to give me a call about that team of hers? I might need to buy them after all." Her voice caught in her throat and she turned and walked away quickly before Jessa could answer.

"You see, you *are* famous," Cheryl said in awe. "*Everybody* knows who you are."

"Grab a shovel," Jessa said. "Let's get to work."

21

That evening, when Jessa was struggling through a book about coal miners at the beginning of the twentieth century, Mrs. Bailey phoned. She was home and finally starting to feel better.

"They plowed the main road properly today," she said. "It's getting pretty wet down here, but I was hoping you might be able to come over for a visit tomorrow. I found something interesting you might find helpful for your homework assignment."

"I'll come by after we take my dad to the airport," Jessa said. She hung up the phone and went upstairs to bed. She could already hear her father's soft snores from the living room couch. Jessa figured he had never laboured so hard in his entire life.

The airport was crowded with people trying to leave the city the next morning.

"Jessa?" her father said as they waited for his flight to

be called. "Would it be okay if I wrote to you sometimes?"

Jessa blushed and nodded. She had sort of enjoyed the past few days, working side by side with her father. Jessa had to admit he was actually pretty easy to get along with.

"Maybe you could come for another visit sometime—but in the summer," she suggested.

She and her father laughed.

"That would be good," he agreed. He gave her a quick, awkward hug and picked up his carry-on bag.

"In spite of everything, I had fun here," he grinned.

He gave a little wave and then walked away to board his plane.

"Dad?" Jessa called after him. He turned back to look at her.

"Next time you come, you can have my room."

He laughed and winked. "Thanks, Jessa."

And then he was gone.

Jessa's mother gave her shoulder a squeeze, and they turned and walked out of the airport together.

Mrs. Bailey spread the old newspaper out on the dining room table. In 1958 the *Victoria Daily Times* had published a special centennial edition. The headline on the front page read

B.C.'s First Hundred Years

"Maybe you can get some ideas from this."

Jessa sat down at the table. The paper was yellowed and worn and the old-fashioned drawings on the front page were faded.

"July 15, 1958," Jessa read slowly.

Mrs. Bailey turned the first page.

Gold Fever Madness Gave Birth to B.C.

"It would have been so exciting to have lived during the Gold Rush," Jessa said.

She read aloud from the article. "*The gold fever became a madness. Men suffered and swore, sweated and froze, fought Indians and privation.* Privation? What's that?" Jessa asked.

"Making do without the necessities of life," said Mrs. Bailey. "We have it pretty easy these days, even though we like to complain a lot."

"Oh, look!" said Jessa, pointing to a photo of an old woman with a wide, cheerful smile. "She was born way back in 1864!" Jessa skimmed through the article about the woman, one of Victoria's pioneers.

"She brought her piano ashore on the front of an Indian war canoe!"

"She would have been alive when the legislature buildings were finished in 1898," said Mrs. Bailey.

Jessa loved the turrets and domes of Victoria's legislature. At night, when all its twinkling lights were lit, the place looked more like a palace out of a picture book than a place where the government met.

"You could write about Frances Rattenbury—the architect who designed the building."

"Architects are boring," said Jessa.

"Not *this* one. Rattenbury was a great scoundrel! Did you know he was murdered when his wife's boyfriend clubbed him over the head with a mallet?"

"Really?" Jessa asked.

"Oh, yes. Not only that, when Mrs. Rattenbury found out what had happened to her husband, she stabbed herself in the stomach and then threw herself into a river, just to make doubly sure she was dead, I suppose."

"Wow," said Jessa. She turned her attention back to the

old newspaper. On the bottom half of the page was a photo of four draft horses hitched to a strange-looking cart.

"Look at this! They're pulling a twenty-ton steel beam that was used to build the Victoria High School."

Jessa turned the pages gingerly. She was afraid the fragile paper would tear.

"How am I going to choose just one person to write about?" she groaned.

"Does your project have to be about just one person?"

Jessa thought a moment. "Hey," she said. "I just had an idea!"

Mrs. Bailey looked at Jessa over the top of her reading glasses.

"I know exactly what I'm going to do for my project!" Her words tumbled out as she explained everything to Mrs. Bailey. When Jessa finally stopped talking, Mrs. Bailey's eyes were twinkling.

"Look!" Jessa said, waving a postcard of Mickey and Minnie Mouse in front of Cheryl. "Look what I got from Jeremy!"

Cheryl took the card from Jessa and sat down at her desk. Jessa fidgeted beside her. "Hurry up! Mrs. Glocken will be here any second."

Cheryl dropped her jaw in exaggerated amazement as she read the message on the back. "Oooooh!" she squealed. "Jeremy wrote to you! He really wrote to you!"

Jessa flushed. She knew she was beaming but she couldn't help it. Jeremy had actually written to *her*.

"Here she comes," she said as Mrs. Glocken came into the classroom. Jessa snatched the card back and turned it over. She read it for the hundredth time.

Dear Jessa,

California is really warm. We stayed in a hotel on a pier sticking over the ocean. It would have been a lot of fun to take Caspian and Rebel on a gallop along the sandy beaches here. I can't wait to get home. I miss riding Caspian.

Bye, Jeremy

Jessa slipped her precious mail inside the front cover of her math book and forced herself to concentrate on what Mrs. Glocken was saying.

At the end of class, everyone began collecting their books.

"Jessa? Don't forget, I need to see you after class," said Mrs. Glocken.

Rachel's eyebrows shot up and she leaned over to whisper something to Sarah. Jessa just smiled knowingly. She was putting her plan into effect. Her meeting with Mrs. Glocken was just phase one. The others would see soon enough what was happening.

"So, are you failing socials?" Rachel asked at lunch. She was clearly dying to know why Jessa had stayed behind after the others had been dismissed.

Jessa drained her carton of chocolate milk.

"It must be serious," speculated Monika. "You missed part of math class."

"Really. It was nothing," started Jessa. But she didn't have time to say another word because a hush fell over the table and all eyes turned to stare at the woman who had come up behind Jessa.

Jessa turned around slowly and looked up.

"Oh! Mrs. Dereks," she said in shock. She hadn't expected the school principal to be looming over her.

"Jessa," she said coolly. "Do you have a minute to meet with me in my office?"

"Right now?"

Mrs. Dereks nodded, and Jessa obediently pushed her chair back from the table. All eyes watched her rise and follow tall, stern Mrs. Dereks across the cafeteria. She could feel her friends' horrified stares on the back of her neck. She could just imagine what they were saying.

Jessa smiled to herself. No matter how inventive their explanations, they would never guess why she had been called into Mrs. Dereks' office. Jessa had even managed to keep her plan a secret from Cheryl.

"Please bring your journal assignments to the front of the class," said Mrs. Glocken on Friday.

Everyone except Jessa handed their assignments to Mrs. Glocken.

"Jessa? Where's yours?" whispered Cheryl.

"Shhh."

"Didn't you get it finished?"

Jessa pretended she didn't hear her friend's question. Cheryl wasn't the only one who had noticed.

"Hey, Richardson. Didn't get your homework done?" Rachel asked.

It was getting very hard to ignore Rachel's pointed comments.

"Of course she did," said Cheryl. "Didn't you?"

"Are you going to do a play?" Rachel asked Cheryl.

"No," said Cheryl. "Monika and I decided to do separate projects because we couldn't get together over the holidays. It snowed, you know."

Jessa didn't say anything, but she happened to know Monika and Cheryl had kept arguing about who was going to do what in the play. The blizzard was just a very convenient excuse.

"I wrote a journal about a girl who lives in England and falls in love with a Frenchman who teaches landscape painting," Cheryl said.

"Quiet, girls! Back to your desks. Jessa? Perhaps you'd like to come to the front of the class and explain why you haven't handed in an assignment?"

Cheryl's eyes bulged and Rachel's head swivelled as she turned to try to catch the expression on Jessa's face.

Jessa ignored everyone and walked to the front of the classroom.

Mrs. Glocken waited expectantly.

Jessa's heart pounded. She hoped she would find the right words to explain.

"As you might know, I really like horses," Jessa started. She heard a few giggles. "A hundred years ago, horses were as common as cars. They were used to pull fire trucks, haul building supplies, and take families shopping, to piano lessons and school."

Jessa cleared her throat. "Unfortunately, horses don't keep journals. But, unlike the people who lived in the nineteenth century, horses are still around and doing what they did back then." Jessa looked over at Mrs. Glocken, who stood up behind her desk and spoke.

"Class, if you'll all quietly file out to the front of the school, Jessa will introduce you to two special guests."

Harpo and Markus looked gorgeous standing outside in the sunshine. They were hitched to an old-fashioned wooden wagon driven by Roslyn Anderson. She waved when she saw Jessa coming out of the school.

Mrs. Dereks was talking to Mrs. Bailey beside the

wagon. She was holding a stack of papers.

"Jessa! Here—I made the photocopies, as requested. What lovely horses!"

Jessa beamed. She stood in front of the wagon and cleared her throat. Her classmates gathered around Harpo and Markus.

"In the olden days, horses would have been used to deliver things. Like newspapers," she said loudly, continuing her speech.

Jessa held up the top sheet on the pile of photocopies. The fancy banner across the top read

The Victoria Gazette

The lead story was about another snowstorm, one which had paralyzed the city of Victoria nearly a hundred years earlier. She handed each student a copy of the newspaper she had laboured so hard to make. It had taken a whole evening on her mother's computer to get it to look just right.

"A newspaper is a journal for a whole city," she said. "In my paper you can read all about pioneers, fur traders, gold seekers, and architects who were alive in the early days of British Columbia. In many of the stories the noble horse played an important role."

Mrs. Dereks stood beside Jessa.

"A hundred years from now," she said, "maybe someone will do a school project and read an article about you and *these* two horses who were such heroes in the blizzard."

Jessa blushed. Mrs. Bailey gave her a broad wink.

"Anybody want a ride in the wagon?" she asked. Every hand in the class shot up. Jessa climbed up onto the driver's seat beside Roslyn and took the reins.

"Six at a time, please," Jessa said. When her first load of passengers was settled she raised the lines and let them fall lightly on the two golden horses in front of her.

"Come on, boys. Git up!"

Books by Nikki Tate
Available from Sono Nis Press

The StableMates Series

StableMates 1: *Rebel of Dark Creek*
StableMates 2: *Team Trouble at Dark Creek*
StableMates 3: *Jessa Be Nimble, Rebel Be Quick*
StableMates 4: *Sienna's Rescue*
StableMates 5: *Raven's Revenge*
StableMates 6: *Return to Skoki Lake*
StableMates 7: *Keeping Secrets at Dark Creek*

The Tarragon Island Series

Tarragon Island
No Cafés in Narnia

The Estorian Chronicles

Book One: *Cave of Departure*
Book Two: *The Battle for Carnillo*

Photo: E.Colin Williams

About the Author

Nikki Tate lives in Victoria, British Columbia and is a much sought after workshop leader who is entertaining, inspiring, and informative. She enjoys working with young aspiring writers and has spoken to thousands of school children across Canada and the United States about the writing process. All of Tate's novels have received consistently positive reviews and have appeared on the BC Bestseller list time and time again.

Visit Nikki's website at:
www.stablemates.net